# FINDING MILDRED

a novel by

Norman Reed Paterson

FriesenPress
Suite 300 - 990 Fort St
Victoria, BC, Canada, V8V 3K2
www.friesenpress.com

**Copyright © 2015 by Norman Reed Paterson**
First Edition — 2015

Places mentioned in this book are, for the most part, correctly named and placed in their proper locations. Street-names and principal features are more or less as they should be. Certain establishments such as restaurants, retirement homes and schools are entirely fictitious, as the author is anxious not to offend or overly flatter owners or occupants.

An exception to this scheme of things is the town called Orchard Bay, in which much of the action takes place. Residents of, or visitors to, southern Georgian Bay may recognize some similarity between the town and a number of villages in the region. However, all of the characters and events described in the book are entirely fictitious.

All rights reserved.

No part of this publication may be reproduced in any form, or by any means, electronic or mechanical, including photocopying, recording, or any information browsing, storage, or retrieval system, without permission in writing from FriesenPress.

**ISBN**
978-1-4602-7454-5 (Hardcover)
978-1-4602-7455-2 (Paperback)
978-1-4602-7456-9 (eBook)

*1. Fiction, Mystery & Detective*

Distributed to the trade by The Ingram Book Company

# CHAPTER 1

If Leonard were the sort of person who planned things ahead, he would know that he couldn't possibly complete his walk before dark, and would therefore not be in his present predicament. Instead, here he is, not yet out of the woods, stumbling on the rough trail and peering ahead for the opening that will lead him to the road and, eventually, home. Morgan, who has been running ahead, turns and barks encouragingly. He has been through this before. Eventually, Leonard makes his way out of the trees and is astonished to find, directly in front of him, a newly constructed two-story house surrounded by unlandscaped, excavated earth, where in past years the path used to cross a short strip of grass bordering the road. Morgan, with his customary disregard for property boundaries, keeps straight on, narrowly skirting the building. Leonard, temporarily baffled and roundly cursing a landowner who would build a house across a public right-of-way, takes a more circuitous route. He is so pre-occupied with the injustice of the thing that he almost misses seeing the face that appears then disappears in an upstairs window. He has a sudden urge to confront the owner of the face and get an explanation for the outrage, but decides instead to use the remaining daylight to complete his way home. Calling Morgan, who has taken an interest in the front door of the house, he continues at a more rapid pace that will take him the final kilometre to his home. Morgan, a medium-sized brown dog who is obedient when it suits him, puts dinner ahead of curiosity and joins his owner along the road.

Opening the front door of the bungalow that he shares with his wife Shirley, Leonard loses no time in making his feelings known.

"Hello, Shirl! Guess what! Someone's built a damn great house on Jacob Way right where the River Trail comes out onto the road."

"What's this about?" A blond, rather harassed-looking woman emerges from the kitchen, grabbing a towel to wipe the mud from Morgan's feet.

"You know, where you cross the field to get to the road—they've put up an ugly two-story house. Must have been done while we were away last winter."

"They can't do that; it's a public trail." Shirley is as surprised as Leonard and, though not as keen a walker as her husband, appreciates the network of trails that thread their neighbourhood.

Leonard vows to visit the Town Hall and get the matter cleared up, and the subject is dropped for the moment. One thought does come across his mind, however: *There was something wrong with the face at the window. Was it startled? Afraid? Vulnerable?* He picks up the phone. "Jack. How are things? Hey—what's with this new house on Jacob Way, right in the middle of the River Trail?"

Leonard Stevenson and Jack Miller (and their wives and animals) live in a small Ontario town called Orchard Bay. If you were taken there blindfolded, you could be excused for thinking you were in a suburb of Toronto—except, that is, when you are on the main street or the street crossing it, in which case the circa 1880s buildings, now mostly boutiques and restaurants, would place you squarely in a country village largely populated by retirees and weekenders.

Jack, in his younger years, sold products for a large pharmaceutical company, which explains why he has the answer to any question you ask him. Not *an* answer, but *the* answer. And that is why Leonard, who is a retired lawyer and is not absolutely certain of anything, phones Jack when he wants to be put straight.

"Yes," says Jack, "they started building that house last December and the folks moved in in March. Not bad, considering the weather. What's the problem?"

"It's built across the bloody River Trail, that's what."

"They own the land apparently—not just where the house is, but for miles on each side. The woman who lives there doesn't like you to cross her property."

"But I thought that that trail was on public land."

"Apparently not. It's only public up to the edge of the woods. If you don't want to upset the owner you have to find your way through the bush up to the Twenty-fourth Sideroad and then down Jacob Way. Takes you another fifteen minutes at least—possibly more."

"Well, that's ridiculous. The Trails Committee should have been told when they built that part of the trail." Leonard pauses. "I would have thought that the public would have right-of-passage given that there was no objection up till now. I'm going to check with Town Hall."

# CHAPTER 2

CHARLOTTE draws her head in quickly. Since she is technically in the house illegally it might not be a good thing to be seen there at this point. She has made the journey by car from Toronto, expecting to be welcomed by Aunt Mildred on arrival in the village. Instead, she found the door unlocked but no one at home and no note.

Charlotte has not seen her aunt for at least twenty years. As a child she remembers Christmas parties in Hamilton where her father Jim Prosser worked as a foreman at the steel plant. At age eight her mental picture of Aunt Mildred, Jim's sister, is that of a rather shy woman with glasses and a smelly wool cardigan. She was a schoolteacher, Charlotte remembers. Unmarried, but kind—which is what Charlotte needs now. Jim died in a plant accident a year after Charlotte married, so at least he was spared the drawn-out misery that she went through with her husband Graham Fox. "Foxy," her father had called him, a name that as time went on Charlotte realized was pretty appropriate. "Wolfy," really—he certainly had the appetite of a wolf—and he drained her physically, emotionally, and now financially. Well, she is rid of Graham and has taken to calling herself Charlotte Prosser again. And in her new, unmarried but still emotionally fragile state she has turned to Aunt Mildred for comfort and (possibly) a place to hang out until she can find a job and move on to a new chapter in her life.

Charlotte phoned before driving to Orchard Bay and Aunt Mildred seemed vague but prepared to put her up for a while at least. She explained to Charlotte that she had just moved in and that things in the house were a bit of a mess. But Charlotte was not prepared for what she found—a house not only empty of an owner, but of almost everything else. Downstairs the only rooms that had any furniture were the dining room (an IKEA table and four chairs) and a sort of sunroom which boasted a huge plush sofa, an armchair, and a bookcase with family photos, a few of which she thought she recognized. Upstairs, Aunt Mildred seemed to have unpacked in a hurry as one bedroom was full of half-empty suitcases and another just a bed and a dresser. Charlotte supposes she will spend the night on the plush sofa.

The third bedroom is empty and Charlotte opens the window and looks out. She sees a man and a dog, and ducks quickly back in. She is not anxious to advertise her arrival. She returns downstairs and waits for the dog to vacate the front porch then fetches her belongings from the car. The car, a ten-year-old Volkswagen and the only significant item that survived her marriage break-up, is still sitting on the street as she has not found a way of opening the garage. She dumps her belongings in the front hall and retires to the plush sofa to consider her next step. Right—call Aunt Mildred on her cell.

"Hi—is that you, Aunt Mildred? It's Charlotte. I'm in your house—okay. Where do I put my things? No problem, see you." Charlotte hangs up. She wonders why Aunt Mildred would choose this moment to get her hair done, but she is a not a person that looks for problems and sets about putting her clothes in the cupboard in the third bedroom.

When Aunt Mildred drives up some time later and opens the front door Charlotte sees a large, late-middle-aged, rather intimidating woman with what is clearly a very recently coiffed hairdo. Brassy is how Charlotte would describe it. Not at all like the Aunt Mildred she remembers. "Well, my dear," pants the older woman, "not a very nice way to welcome you, I'm afraid. Had to get my hair done. Looked awful. Call me Mildred, dear, after all we're almost the same age." Mildred continues a flow of chatter while dumping some groceries on the kitchen counter. Charlotte wonders why she should be classed as nearly the same age as her aunt, who is clearly at least twice her age.

After a hasty supper taken at the IKEA table, Mildred explains what she has been doing for the past twenty years and how Charlotte has suddenly come back into her life. Charlotte's recollection of events, narrated years ago by her father, was that Jim and Mildred were born on a farm in this neighbourhood but moved to Hamilton at an early age with their mother, who did not like farm life. Her grandfather, Jacob Prosser, later sold the farm and joined the family in Hamilton. Mildred became a teacher, and Jim worked for the steel company. Mildred formed an attachment and left Ontario with her partner for Vancouver Island. She did not come back east and more or less lost touch with the family. Mildred's version of this is similar in the essentials but puts the blame on her brother Jim for not keeping in touch. What brings her back to Ontario now is the discovery that she has inherited a twenty-acre parcel of land from her father's estate, and since Jim is long dead she is the sole beneficiary, and she has decided to build on it and move back to this nice part of Ontario.

Charlotte is astonished by this story. She knows that her grandfather was a farmer and had property in this area, but Jim never told her that the family kept some of the land. How long has Mildred known about this inheritance? And why wait until now to claim it?

Mildred explains that she and her partner were happy in British Columbia and had no wish to move. The property was cared for by the farmer who bought the other 180 acres of her grandfather's original holdings, and was appreciating in price. Mildred broke up with her partner recently and it seemed like a good time to move. "I had some money saved up so I looked up builders on the internet, picked a design I liked, and had them build me a house. I think I'm going to like it here. When I got your call a while ago I thought, wouldn't that be nice if my niece were to come and stay with me. You poor dear, I understand you had a disappointing marriage. Perhaps things will improve now."

Charlotte is having a bit of trouble with all this. Why would Mildred not sell the property and use the proceeds to buy some land on sunny Vancouver Island? Why would she not have come east while the house was being built? And where, for goodness sake, is all the furniture?

To the last question, Mildred explains that she decided to sell all her (and her partner's) household possessions in BC and buy new stuff here. "Charlotte, dear, we'll do this together, and the first thing will be a nice bed for you, but tonight you must sleep on the sofa." Charlotte thinks *at least I got one thing right,* but is still a bit uneasy as she retires for the first night in this strange house with this rather odd woman.

# CHAPTER 3

THE Orchard Bay Municipal Offices are housed in a newly built Town Hall, close to the shore of the bay. Leonard Stevenson is fairly familiar with the way things are organized as he has looked into a number of matters for friends, as well as himself, in his role as a retired lawyer. For these favours he asks nothing more than that you laugh at his golf jokes.

He heads for the Planning, Property and By-Law Services office and enquires of Emily, the secretary, if George is available. George is in a Council meeting but will be through in about thirty minutes. This gives Leonard time to visit the room where the lot plans are kept, and he has no trouble locating the map covering the twenty-acre property. He notes that the boundaries of the parcel extend at least five hundred metres north and south of the new house (not "miles" as claimed by Jack Miller, but then some exaggeration is permissible under the circumstances). And he is not surprised to see that no easement is recorded where the River Trail crosses the property. Further examination shows the parcel to be registered in the name Jacob Prosser, who was also the original owner of adjacent lands transferred to an Earl Dean in 1950. The street separating the parcel from the adjacent land is called Jacob Way after the original owner. Leonard knows the Dean family; Marvin Dean is a prosperous apple grower and a curling buddy of Leonard's.

The new house is not registered on the lot map and Leonard needs to go to Building and Permit Services for that information. Meanwhile, George has returned to his office and is willing to handle Leonard's enquiry.

"Nice to see you George, keeping busy and out of trouble?"

George, a very small man with gold-rimmed glasses, is clearly not in the mood for small talk.

"How can I help you, Len?"

"You know the new house on Jacob Way, a few hundred metres north of the Twenty-fourth Sideroad?"

"Yes, and I suppose you are asking why we let them build on the River Trail?"

"As a matter of fact, yes."

"Well, that's easy. There was no easement, so we had no option."

"But surely there are grounds for saying that the trail has been in public use without objection from the owner for quite a few years. Doesn't that constitute grounds for an official right of passage?"

There is some legal discussion between the two men, the outcome being that since nobody came forward at the time the building application was under review, there was no basis for turning it down. Leonard is aware of a slight unease on George's part and interprets this as an acknowledgement that maybe Parks and Recreation Services should have objected or made some effort to have the building location moved a few metres to the north or south. He asks, "Is there no way the trail can be shifted to skirt the house?"

"Apparently the owner of the house is also the owner of the twenty-acre parcel in which it sits, and she is unwilling to allow any easement whatsoever."

"That seems ridiculous. Can you give me her name? Perhaps I can persuade her."

"I suppose I can do that, since you can get it anyway from Building Services. It is Mildred Prosser, apparently old Jacob Prosser's daughter."

Leonard leaves Town Hall with that feeling that many people have after dealing with official bureaucracy. If common sense had prevailed, he feels, some compromise should have been possible. Maybe it is not too late. Leonard is nothing if not an eternal optimist. He believes right will prevail—with a little help—if you use common sense. He has no time for offenders who try and bury their mistakes. A friend once called him and asked his advice about a speeding offence. "I don't have time to go to court," his friend said. Leonard asked him if there were any extenuating circumstance, and when told there were not, asked him why he wanted to go to court. "Well, what should I do?" asked his friend. "Don't speed," was Leonard's reply.

Now, walking away from the Town Hall, Leonard goes over the facts. *There are some questions that need answers,* he thinks. Was there some arrangement on the part of the previous landowner that allowed passage of the trail? Why would the current owner refuse to negotiate an easement on some other part of the property? Who had responsibility for looking after the twenty acres in the absence of the owner? Possibly the neighbour who purchased his land from old Jacob Prosser made some arrangement about access. Marvin Dean might know.

He calls his friend Marvin and they agree to meet for coffee.

# Chapter 4

CHARLOTTE grew up in Hamilton, attending St. Mary Catholic High School to the grade twelve level. She was named Charlotte after her grandmother, Jacob's wife, whose name was Carlotta. Her mother died of cancer when she was fourteen, and Jim Prosser, her dad, did his best to look after her. Since he worked shifts at the steel mill this was not easy, and Charlotte spent a fair amount of time on her own. Her outward appearance was that of a rather immature, vulnerable girl, anxious to please—happy to be included in the pack. Her teachers referred to her as a bright girl with imagination and persistence. These qualities did not always ensure academic success, as Charlotte was often more interested in what was not taught than what was required on the annual examinations. Growing up in a largely immigrant part of the city, she had friends from many different cultures, different tastes, and different goals in life. One of these was Lucy Pears whose father came from England and was with the Hamilton Police Department. She and Lucy were both active, fun-loving teens and Lucy's parents were kind to her on her frequent visits to Lucy's home after school. Both girls were influenced by the stories told by Lucy's dad about life in the police force and both went as far as to enquire about the Police Studies course given at nearby Mohawk College. Jim Prosser was against this, however, and steered Charlotte into a program called Municipal and Justice Services, which could lead to a broader range of careers.

At Mohawk Charlotte fell madly in love with a junior teacher called Graham Fox. They dated briefly, then, at Charlotte's insistence and against her father's advice, got married. Trouble started early and became worse. Graham was lazy, chased after countless other students, and continually borrowed money from Charlotte's meagre resources. He persuaded Charlotte to quit her studies and take a job with a real estate company. After Charlotte threatened to leave he settled down for a while and they even talked about having a child. Then, an unfortunate event happened: Jim Prosser, in an attempt to save a fellow employee who caught his overall sleeve in a rolling mill, was badly hurt, and died shortly after. Charlotte dealt with funeral arrangements and handled the estate matters as best she could. Aunt Mildred sent flowers from British Columbia but said she could not take the time off to come east. An appointed attorney read the will and Charlotte found herself the beneficiary of a surprisingly healthy estate, most of which had been handed down via her father from what he had inherited from old Jacob Prosser. Graham Fox, Charlotte's husband, sensing an unexpected windfall, quit his job at Mohawk and tried to persuade Charlotte to set him up in business. By this time he had added to his problems by drinking heavily and, when drunk, physically abusing his wife. Lucy and her other friends advised her to leave and seek a divorce, but Charlotte persisted in a fruitless attempt to straighten him out. The end came when Graham forged a cheque on Charlotte's account and spent it all on the racetrack. With a good deal of her money gone and a husband convicted of theft, Charlotte decided to look for a job as far away from Hamilton as possible.

Despite her seeming lack of interest in family, Aunt Mildred was the obvious person to turn to and Charlotte wrote to the last address she had for her aunt. After receiving no reply (or a returned letter), she obtained her aunt's phone number from the attorney who dealt with the estate. She was surprised to be met with a cheerful "well it's you, Charlotte; how nice." Mildred told her she had decided to move back to Ontario and was thinking of building a house on the property left to her by her father. If Charlotte could wait until spring she would love to have her come and stay with her in her new house.

It was a gloomy winter for Charlotte but she was able to complete her studies at Mohawk and by April was ready to set forth as Charlotte Prosser on the next phase of her life.

# Chapter 5

WHEN Leonard Stevenson wanted a cup of coffee ten years ago, there was only one place he could find one other than home. The bakery on Main Street produced a reasonable cup and a choice of butter tart, Chelsea bun, or carrot cake. The village did not even have a Tim Hortons. Leonard was once stopped by the driver of an American car and asked, "Can you tell me where the Tim Hortons is?" Not *is* there a Tim Hortons, but *where is it*. It was assumed by American visitors that all Ontario towns and villages had a Tim Hortons.

It was some years after that that Tims actually came to the village, and by that time two other coffee shops of the Starbucks variety had already opened. Now there are probably six places that will serve a cup of very decent coffee without asking, "Are you staying for lunch?"

Leonard enjoys a cup in the morning. Once, when waiting for his car to be fixed, he poured himself a cup from a machine in the waiting room and commented to the receptionist, "I like a heart-starter in the morning." The receptionist, a large black lady, replied in a southern drawl, "When my husband asks for a heart-starter in the morning, he don't mean no cup of coffee."

Leonard is now heading for his favourite establishment, a roastery that imports its coffee directly from East Africa. He is expecting to meet Marvin Dean and discuss the troublesome business of the new house on Jacob Way. The café is small and not ideal for a private conversation, but Leonard is not shy and is the kind of person who never expects other people to be listening to him. Marvin is there waiting. They order coffee.

"Well, Len—what's on your mind?"

"It's the property surrounding the new house on Jacob Way. I know you have the land across the street and I wondered if you knew if there had ever been an easement to allow passage through the property to connect with the River Trail."

"Funny you should ask. I haven't met the new owner yet, but I've been meaning to ask her why she chose that spot when people have been crossing there ever since her dad severed it from the rest of his farm. You know, old Jacob Prosser sold the rest of his farm to my dad Earl."

"Tell me more," said Leonard.

"Well, apparently Jacob wanted the land to be public as it's narrow to use for farming, and he had no personal interest in real estate. He made a deal with Earl that we would look after the place—you know, grow some hay on it, keep it tidy. We get the hay of course. Always kept a path across it for the public to get to the woods. When Jacob died he left the property to his daughter who went out west and never got in touch with my dad or me. I was surprised when she started building there, but it wasn't my business to interfere. Now she's here I think I ought to speak to her about Jacob's arrangement with our family."

Leonard is astonished; he had not expected this. "George, down at the Planning Department, says they asked Mildred—she's the daughter—if she would allow a trail across some distance from the house, and she said no."

"Not surprised—George couldn't persuade a starving dog to eat his dinner."

"But what has she got to lose? She might even be able to squeeze a few bucks out of the Town."

The two men continue on this theme and agree that the questions on Leonard's mind are still unanswered. In fact, if Mildred had known her dad's intentions, which seems likely, why is she acting in this strange manner? They decide that a meeting with Mildred is in order and that Marvin, who is still taking care of the property in the absence of other instructions, has the best excuse for setting this up.

# CHAPTER 6

CHARLOTTE has been a guest at Mildred's house for almost a week and her uneasiness has not really abated. There are moments when she thinks life is normal, like when Mildred gets a landscaper over to discuss turning the battlefield around the house into a garden, or when she and her aunt visit the public library and open accounts so they can borrow books and DVDs. But inside the house there is still chaos. Mildred has not really unpacked. Charlotte's room now has a bed and a bureau, but the spare bedroom is still full of half-emptied and unopened suitcases. They have discussed the financial arrangements and Mildred has told her not to worry. When Charlotte has a job she may move or they can come to some arrangement.

She is astonished when Mildred announces one day that she intends to sell lots on the twenty acres surrounding the house. She wants Charlotte to handle the business for her: speak to agents and find out what real estate is selling for. There could be a lot of money in this market. She hints that the two of them might form a business and that Charlotte, with her training in municipal and legal services, would be well equipped to manage it. Charlotte is pleased with this idea and suggests that when she is able she might like to buy a share. Mildred will hear nothing of this. "After all, child, you are my next of kin."

It is in the middle of these discussions that Mildred receives a phone call. A Marvin Dean introduces himself as a neighbour and owner of Jacob Prosser's old farm and wonders if it would be possible to come over and have a chat. He would like to bring a friend with him who has a possible interest in Mildred's twenty acres. "Would tomorrow after four o'clock be okay?" Mildred has been half expecting this and agrees. Charlotte is happy that they will be meeting neighbours, even if the two men are at least twice her age.

Before the men arrive Mildred takes Charlotte aside and explains that it would be doing her a favour if she, Charlotte, would mind acting as if she is a part-owner of the property and therefore a party to the discussions. Charlotte is surprised but not unwilling.

Around five o'clock the doorbell rings and Charlotte is faced with the two strangers and a dog. There is almost instant recognition on both sides. Charlotte has seen one of the men before and, being there with the dog, brings back at once the location and time of their previous encounter: it was that first evening, when she looked out the upstairs window. On his part, Leonard was prepared to meet the face at the window, although Mildred had said nothing on the phone about a fourth person at their meeting. He politely asks if Morgan can come in but offers to tie him up outside, if that were preferred. Charlotte says Morgan will be welcome. Mildred interrupts and says, "So long as he stays with you; I'm allergic to dogs."

Introductions are made, all parties expressing a wish to be called by their first names, and the four sit down around the IKEA table. Mildred offers tea, which is accepted. Marvin starts the conversation.

"Mildred, I have been wanting to meet you. My dad and yours were such good friends, and it's so nice to have you as a neighbour."

"It is nice to be here—I understand you are still living in Dad's old house."

"Yes, though with some pretty major renovations. What I would like to get settled now is do you want me to continue looking after the land? You know, we had this arrangement that I would take care of it in return for any revenue that I might get from hay or whatever."

"I've been thinking about that, Marvin, and for the time being, if you are willing, I would be very happy. Anyone for more tea?"

Leonard thinks it is time for him to put in a word or two. "I have been wondering, since you built this house, whether you are planning to develop any more of your land."

Charlotte, taking a cue from Mildred's look, enters the conversation. "We have been considering selling some of the land, probably as lots, but we haven't really started along that road yet."

"In that case, could we persuade you to allow our River Trail Committee to find a suitable place for the path to cross the land?" Leonard asks. "We used to cross it at this house, but that's not possible now. I don't think it would interfere with Marvin's looking after the land. I'm a lawyer and I could draft up some sort of agreement if you need it."

Charlotte notices a sudden change in Mildred's demeanour. She gets up from the table when the River Trail is brought up and, at the mention of the word lawyer, turns around and in a shaky voice says, "I don't think that will be necessary."

Marvin speaks up. "Your dad always asked me to leave a path from where the trail comes out of the woods, so folks could get out onto Jacob Way without going all the way up to the Twenty-fourth."

"What Jacob Prosser did was his business and this is mine—and Charlotte's of course," Mildred replies quickly.

Marvin and Leonard know it is time to admit defeat. Leonard adds, "You will give it some thought, won't you Mildred? Morgan and I would be very grateful—won't we, Morgan?"

Morgan wags his tail, which is bushy and probably the best part of his mixed heritage. His lack of pedigree has never bothered Morgan, who takes life as it comes.

After the visitors have left, Charlotte asks her aunt, "Why are you so opposed to having a trail across the land? We can easily build it into a development plan or, if we have an agreement, we can always cancel it if it interferes with the housing."

"I think we have said enough for now," replies Mildred, and leaves the room.

# Chapter 7

WAKING up next day, Charlotte finds that the uneasy feeling she had on her arrival at Mildred's house has returned. Why is her aunt acting like this? How can she work with Mildred if she can't discuss important things with her? A simple thing like this River Trail should be easy to deal with. Those nice men were only acting kindly—or were they? Do they have some agenda she is unaware of? She decides that if she is going to go on living with her aunt she must get things out into the open. Where to start? The River Trail seems to be a catalyst to her aunt's behaviour, and she needs to find out more about that. That Mr. Stevenson—Leonard—seems to know a lot. Perhaps he would show her the trail. She phones him.

"Mister Stevenson—sorry, Leonard—it's Charlotte. I've been thinking, and I wonder if you could find time to show me the River Trail. I could meet you somewhere. How long? Oh, I don't mind walking for two hours. Do I need boots? No? I'll be at the Filtration Plant at one o'clock—thanks."

Shirley is not the jealous type, but when Leonard tells her he is taking a twentysomething female for a hike around the River Trail, he has some explaining to do. "Honey, if she can influence the Prosser woman to give us an easement, it will be worth it. Besides, Morgan will be there as chaperone."

The Filtration Plant is a fairly modern sewage treatment facility that handles waste for quite a large area along Georgian Bay. There are two settling ponds behind the buildings that take the treated waste and aerate it before returning the water to the lake. If the ponds have any taste or odour the birds are certainly unaware of it. There are never fewer than a dozen gulls, Canada geese, or mallards swimming there happily. They have also done a good job with landscaping and the trail is awarded a small parking lot and a picnic table.

Leonard arrives and parks next to Charlotte's Volkswagen. "How far do you want to go?" he asks. Charlotte has all afternoon and is anxious to see the whole picture. "If you have time, I'd like to go right around."

They set off in a sort of counter-clockwise direction so that they will emerge from the wooded area, right at the critical part—the Prosser home. The trail takes them north to the lake, along the lakefront, past the marina, up a narrow, stream-filled gully where salmon come to spawn in the spring, south past two new developments (the town soccer fields and the cemetery), then roughly east to where the trail arrives at the river—a fast-flowing stream that, with its tributaries, drains a broad valley as far inland as thirty kilometres or so. The trail along the river requires several crossings at bridges and finally enters a large, wooded area and, eventually, a steep climb up the bank to the path where Leonard found himself early in this story. This journey, roughly ten kilometres in length, brings Leonard and Charlotte to the back of the Prosser house. While they have been walking they have made some tentative probes into the question of right-of-ways and now Leonard is able to say, "Here we are at the point where the trail used to pass directly through your building lot. You can see that there is no way to get onto Jacob Way without crossing your land. A hiker would have to fight his way through the woods and back up to the Twenty-fourth Sideroad, and that would add at least two kilometres to the trail."

Charlotte can see the dilemma clearly. "We seem to have reached a sort of impasse."

"If you are worried about the trail getting in the way of future building lots, we could make an agreement that would allow you to cancel at any time."

"Seems to me that Mildred doesn't want a formal agreement, for some reason."

"Well, it could be just a memorandum. I could draw it up."

Charlotte has enjoyed her walk and is looking forward to finishing it, but she is certain Mildred is watching from a back window and is unsure of what to do next. "Come with me," she says finally, taking a course around the house on its north side and continuing on Jacob Way to where the trail enters the woods on the other side. They end up back at their cars without discussing the issue further. Charlotte says she will talk to Mildred, though she has a feeling that this will not do any good.

When she gets home she finds her aunt agitated and affronted. "I saw you with that man and his dog, and you took him right across my land, which I had expressly forbidden."

"I'm sorry, Mildred, but how were we to get to the road without crossing the land?"

"You should have thought of that before starting."

Mildred is clearly upset and Charlotte, who is essentially a kind person, does her best to calm her down while explaining that they really owe the public some sort of compromise.

"After all, Grandfather did allow the trail to cross the land, and people have been used to it—and they can't use that part of the trail any more unless they can somehow get to Jacob Way."

She senses that Mildred is more upset about her taking matters into her own hands than with the real issue. She apologizes for not telling Mildred she was exploring the trail with Leonard, and the matter is dropped.

A day or so later Mildred is washing dishes when she suddenly turns to Charlotte and says, "What would happen if we just ignored what is going on? Leonard or whoever could put up a sign saying 'trail continues on the north side of this lot', and after a week or two people would get used to going around on that side. We wouldn't be giving them permission, and if we wanted to later we could simply put up a fence."

"I think that's a wonderful idea. Do you mind if I bounce it off Leonard?"

"Okay, but remember, I'm not signing anything."

Leonard is pleased to hear that some progress is being made. He suggests that the landscapers either erect a fence or plant a hedge to mark the lot boundary. Charlotte is not sure Mildred will go for this. Leonard says he will see if the Town will spring some funds in the interest of getting the matter sorted out.

# CHAPTER 8

GEORGE in Planning refers Leonard to Parks and Recreation. "After all, they built the trail and didn't bother checking to see if they had right-of-way."

Parks and Recreation has a new boss, Paul, who says that it is not his fault that his predecessor goofed and, anyway, there are no funds for fencing a private property. Leonard tries a little threat, something he has had success with before. "There might be some adverse public opinion—you know, letters to the editor, etc."

"We are running a Town, not a popularity contest," Paul replies.

Leonard now has the bit in his teeth. He calls Claude, chairman of the River Trail Committee, a joint committee of both municipal and volunteer members. He fills him in on the situation and Claude is delighted that Leonard has made some headway with Mildred Prosser. "Leave Paul to me," he says.

Anticipating that Paul's answer will be negative, and aware that Claude cannot raise funds from his committee, Leonard starts to draft a letter to the *Valley Herald*. The acceptance record of this weekly newspaper for unsolicited letters is close to 100%, but it continues to have a good readership, including the folks at Town Hall.

*Dear Editor,*

*Area residents will be dismayed to find that they can no longer use the River Trail without a lengthy and awkward bypass. By granting a building permit to the owner of Lot No. 3004 on Jacob Way, the Town has effectively blocked passage from the woods on the west side of Jacob Way to the street itself. Hikers must now scramble through the woods for almost a kilometre to the Twenty-fourth Sideroad and then over a kilometre back to where they would have come out on Jacob Way, unless they want to turn around and make their way back to where they have come from.*

*The Planning Department claims that there was no public objection to the construction on Lot No. 3004 so it was allowed to proceed. However, the right-of-way that existed through the centre of the lot was not shown on the plan accompanying the public notice.*

*This is another case of neglect on the part of the municipal authorities, and one that calls for rectification at the earliest possible date.*

*Leonard Stevenson*

*Member, River Trail Committee*

Leonard has written similar letters to the *Valley Herald* a number of times in the past on issues such as zoning infractions, garbage pick-up, illegal water-taking, and so on. In general, the authorities ignore them, but sometimes they hit a raw nerve and something gets done. This time he decides to show the letter to Charlotte and Mildred before sending it to the paper. He would not want to upset the somewhat tentative arrangement that Mildred has offered, which stipulated no formal agreement.

Calling Charlotte, he reads the letter to her and is surprised by the vehemence of her reaction. "Leonard, you must be nuts. Mildred would hit the roof if she read that in the paper. She is paranoid about privacy. We'll get the lot boundary clearly marked—posts or vegetation or something—so there is no chance of trespass."

Leonard is disappointed—he thought it was rather a good letter—but his optimism returns when he considers that, at worst, they have a temporary arrangement, and one that will hopefully lead to a permanent easement at some time in the future. He calls Claude to see if there is any change of heart in Parks and Recreation and is not surprised to learn that Paul is still stubbornly refusing to help financially. He decides to take Morgan for a walk and get the matter out of his head.

# CHAPTER 9

LEONARD has lived a fairly conventional life, but he cannot be called a conventional person. Born in Toronto and educated at a private school, he obtained a Bachelor of Science degree (Honours) in Maths and Physics before switching to law at Osgoode Hall. If one was to conclude that this was part of a career plan one would be wrong. Leonard is not a long-term planner. He took Maths and Physics because he was curious about how things work and without consideration of where it might lead him. He found, on graduation, that he was not really interested in research or teaching—the only avenues (other than sales) that were immediately open to him. Law appealed chiefly because his father was a lawyer and Leonard had been fascinated by some of the stories that were aired over the dinner table. He was determined to get into that part of law that sees that wrongs are righted and justice is done. He articled at his father's firm, a small partnership, and eventually became a partner himself. He was a successful litigator, but his career was somewhat hampered by his determination to take on unwinnable cases and to do pro bono work if he felt the cause was a good one. His wife Shirley, who was of a more practical mind and had her heart set on a condo in Florida or California, called him Champion of Lost Causes and the Don Quixote of the Bar.

Shirley married Leonard after he graduated from Osgoode. She was an attractive girl who, like many other nurses in training, found that she was not keen on spending the rest of her life in a hospital. When

Leonard proposed to her, after a fraternity party, she was flattered but a bit taken aback. She had known him for less than a year and had not been aware that he had that sort of thing in mind. She sensed that Leonard was impulsive, but there was no doubt that he was a clever man, whom she liked; and she could do a lot worse. They married, had a brief honeymoon, and then Shirley returned to her nursing course to complete her degree. She took the first job offer, which was a good one, at Sick Kids Hospital. She loved children and dogs and pretty soon had one of each. After the birth of Andrew, Leonard persuaded her to stay at home and be a full-time mother. A second son and then a girl followed in short order. The family moved into a large house in North Toronto and, like many families in the area, settled into a life of kids, schools, and holidays in Muskoka while coping with traffic, illnesses, and arguments. They also enjoyed sports (both Leonard and Shirley were keen golfers and tennis players, and the kids threw themselves into a whole range of team sports), family parties, and outings into the country. Reminded of his own childhood, Leonard insisted on a sit-down dinner (without smartphones) for everyone every night. He and Shirley used this time to encourage conversation on topics of general interest.

The kids grew up and went their own ways, presenting no really serious problems to their parents. Andrew went into law (at the family firm); Charles became an engineer and showed an aptitude for research, leading to postgraduate studies at UBC and then MIT. Kitty was not a good scholar but was persuaded to enrol at Dalhousie, which offered a course in Plant and Animal Sciences. Kitty's interests were focused on the outdoors and, from an early age, her hobbies centred around butterflies, turtles, and pet hamsters. Also, Dalhousie was known for its generous student social amenities and was respectably—but not too obviously—far from her parents. Upon graduation, she answered an advertisement for a position with the Ministry of the Environment in Victoria, BC, and is currently a junior wildlife protection officer, seconded to the Royal Victoria Museum to assist in setting up an exhibit on the "Threatened Species of British Columbia."

Leonard spent long hours aiding wronged clients and attending seminars on environmental law, in which he took a particular interest. Shirley found that doing committee work was frustrating and, while volunteering at the North York Hospital, found time to become a really good bridge player.

One day at dinner Leonard announced that he was tired of practicing law in Toronto and that the firm had agreed to support an office for him in a provincial town where he could practice environmental law. This was a bit tough on Shirley, who had her bridge friends and other connections, but she could see that her husband was in need of a move. They went first to Owen Sound, which was a springboard to a variety of interesting legal cases involving water, wind power, and a host of conservation issues. Leonard joined a number of local conservation groups and found himself doing more and more pro bono work. After several years—during which the Owen Sound office was busy but losing money—by tacit agreement with his partners, Leonard agreed to officially retire. He and Shirley had some close friends in Orchard Bay, a smaller community on the lake, not far from Owen Sound, where there was a good choice of golf courses and where, Shirley was told, she could join any number of serious bridge clubs. They are well settled in when this story starts.

# CHAPTER 10

ONE of the things that Charlotte has learned during her stay with Mildred is to not ask questions. That is to say: questions about the past, the family, likes and dislikes—quite a lot of things, really. Although life is still moving along: a garage has been added, Charlotte has found a job at the library, and Mildred has joined a Keep Fit class in the local Community Centre. Charlotte still feels uncomfortable about living with her aunt, which is a disappointment to her, as she had been looking forward to some friendship—love?—and understanding after her disastrous marriage to Graham. But nothing has really changed domestically. Mildred has still not unpacked, they still lack living room furniture, no one has been invited over for a meal (Charlotte tried once and Mildred vetoed it), and conveniences such as bookshelves, reading lights, and even shower mats are lacking. One more thing disturbs her: Mildred emphatically refuses to talk about her life in Hamilton or British Columbia. A thought comes into her head from time to time—is she really my aunt? She dismisses it because it is not a nice thought and because she asks herself, "Why would someone who is not a close relative invite me into her house?" But the thought persists and she finally decides to deal with it. She has to learn more about her aunt's early life.

Travelling to British Columbia is out of the question, but Charlotte has a friend, Lucy, who is now working for the police department in Hamilton. Mildred spent most of her early life there. She has no idea where they lived, and her father, Jim, kept no family records or photo albums. But surely, there must be some record somewhere of the old Prosser family residence, and a neighbour might still be alive. She and Lucy used to play police games, including "Missing Persons" where they had to search for clues of abductions and absconding husbands.

She waits for Mildred to leave the house and phones the number she has for Lucy, who is now married and has a small child. "Lucy, is that you? It's Charlotte."

"Char, hey—how are things?"

"Fine, Luce, I'm living with my aunt still and have a job at the local library. And I'm over that jerk Graham. How are things, and how's the kid?"

"Good, all round. Why the call?" Lucy likes to come to the point.

"Luce, I may be in trouble and I need your help." Charlotte goes on to explain the doubts she has about Mildred and asks if Lucy would be able to put her on track to finding something about her early life.

"It's possible. I'm working in Support Services and I have access to the Records Business Centre. Give me something to go on." Charlotte tells her about her doubts.

Lucy agrees to look into the matter and phone (Charlotte does not want email) when she has something.

Charlotte feels as if an enormous load has been lifted from her back. She must have been worrying subconsciously about this for a long time. She wants to run and shout and tell someone about it. "Wait—Leonard expressed doubts about Mildred . . . no, it's too soon for that."

# Chapter 11

LUCY works in the Central Police Station in downtown Hamilton and her training at Mohawk College has given her a responsible position. She is able to find out rapidly that the police, at least in Hamilton, do not keep records on private citizens unless they are classified as "offenders." She is not reporting an offence, but it is worth checking to see if either Jacob or Mildred Prosser are listed. They are not. Births, deaths, and marriages are the domain of the Province and she would have to apply to the Office of the Registrar General. She goes online and is directed to the Archives of Ontario. There, she finds that one is only able to order copies of one's own certificate, not others'. She wonders whether the problem facing Charlotte is serious enough to pass on to Investigative Services. She would not want that department contacting Mildred directly, which would put Charlotte in a very difficult spot. She decides to phone Charlotte and report her lack of progress. "No luck, Char, so far. Do you want me to keep trying?"

"Only if you have a bright idea we haven't thought of. I'll see if I can dig up something about schools without making Mildred suspicious." She is nervous about calling the schools in Hamilton in case word gets back to Mildred.

Charlotte was at work at the library the next day when something happened that opened the door to a new approach. Browsing through a stack of books that had been taken off the shelves for possible destruction, she came across a pile of old telephone books. Apparently, libraries in Ontario were at one time required to keep current area phone books on the active shelves, and to store them for at least ten years. Someone had been either lazy or unaware of the rules, as there were phone books going back at least twenty years. What if? She calls Lucy again and asks her to see if the Hamilton Public Library has by any chance kept old phone books, and for how far back. Mildred moved out west about twenty years ago.

Another thought occurs to her: Mildred and Jim must have gone to kindergarten in this village while they were still living on the farm. Would it do any good to dig up memories of a small child? But it could explain why she is so anxious not to meet her contemporaries, who might remember what the real Mildred looked like at age five or six. Charlotte is surprised that Mildred joined a fitness class under the circumstances.

And again—what about the church? Jacob and Carlotta were devout Catholics. St. Mary's would have records of christenings and confirmations. Someone at the church might remember the two Prosser kids. She would look into this, but she has to be careful.

St. Mary's Church is located in a neighbouring village and has a reputation for being very hospitable to itinerant Mexican apple-pickers. The church has a new priest who is anxious to be helpful and has no difficulty digging up records of the two christenings. He gives Charlotte the names of two elderly local women who have been coming to the church for many years. She has no luck with the first woman, who has difficulty remembering back five years—certainly not fifty. The other woman thinks she remembers the Prossers, but cannot recall there being any small kids.

A small breakthrough occurs a few days later. Lucy calls and tells her she has found an address and phone number for Jacob and Carlotta Prosser. The Hamilton Public Library only kept phone books for the regulation ten years, but an older woman at the library remembered a Carlotta Prosser who used to borrow books from the library, and was able to locate the Prossers in an old address book. The woman knew that Carlotta had children, but nothing more than that. Lucy offers to pay a visit to the address on her day off and ask some questions of the neighbours.

That evening Lucy calls Charlotte, breathless with excitement. "I have found a woman who has been living in a house on the same street as the Prossers for nearly fifty years. And she remembers the whole family."

"Wow," is all Charlotte can come up with. And then, after checking to make sure Mildred is not within earshot, "Did you ask her any questions, or should I come down and talk to her?"

"I think that would be best. You are a Prosser and she would be more likely to open up to you than to me."

"Thank you so much, Luce. What do you say I drive down on Saturday—we could have lunch and then we could go around together, if you have time."

"Good, Char, I'd like to come. I'll give her a call and set up a time. See you around noon?"

At last, things are moving. Now Charlotte has to find some excuse for asking questions about her aunt. Probably the best way to approach it would be to say that Mildred has been out west for twenty-odd years and has not kept in contact. Now, she (Charlotte) is anxious to find her and would appreciate any suggestions as to who might have stayed in touch with her. This might draw a blank, but they could go on exchanging memories of her aunt and, in the course, dig up information of importance, such as habits or personal preferences. She might even have a photo or two. All this has to be done very carefully.

She tells Mildred that she is going to visit an old friend in Hamilton and, early Saturday morning, sets off in the Volkswagen on the three-hour journey. They meet at Lucy's house and Charlotte is introduced to Lucy's husband and two small children. Ben, a police officer himself, has agreed to look after the children, and the girls set off to a nearby restaurant. During lunch they discuss their strategy and Lucy agrees that the small lie that Charlotte has invented will be a good start. The woman, it seems, is about Mildred's age and is likely to have some information of value.

Edith Schmidt, the Prossers' neighbour, lives on East 33rd Street near Macassa Park, where she or her husband walk their Schnauzer twice a day. Their home is not close to the Stelco plant, which is where her husband works, and where Jim, Charlotte's father, spent his working years, but it is a pleasant, treed area which is probably why Jacob and Carlotta chose it when they moved to Hamilton. Charlotte is unfamiliar with the neighbourhood. She was born and grew up on Maplewood Avenue, only three blocks from Stelco.

The Schmidt home is a modest house but very well maintained and with a nice front garden. Edith is a slight woman, seventyish, with her hair neatly arranged. She is obviously eager to be of assistance and invites the two visitors into the living room. Introductions are made. Herman is off-shift and joins the group. Lucy starts the conversation.

"Charlotte and I grew up together in Hamilton and she called me a week or so ago to see if I could help her locate her aunt Mildred Prosser. I work for the Police Department and she thought that automatically made me an expert on missing persons." This brings a weak laugh, which is good because the mention of police was perhaps unwise. "I traced the Prossers through an address book belonging to a woman who works at the Public Library—quite by accident, really. And then I was lucky to find you people on almost the first try."

"What Herman and I would like to know is why your friend is trying to locate her aunt, and how Mildred became missing," replies Edith.

"I can explain that," says Charlotte. "Mildred apparently went out west with a friend about twenty years ago, when I was about eight years old. She was not close to my dad, Jim, and did not bother to keep in touch. Dad died about ten years ago in an accident at the steel plant and left nothing in the way of address books or phone numbers."

"I remember that accident," Herman interrupts. "I was at the plant at the time. I'm sorry."

Charlotte continues, "I have been going over some estate matters and I need to contact Mildred regarding some property she was apparently left up north by Grandfather Prosser. The only clue I have is that she apparently told Dad that she and her partner were going to live on Vancouver Island."

"Well," says Edith, "I don't think we can help much. We knew the Prossers well and Mildred was quite a good friend of mine—you know, school and stuff—and she told us she was going out west. We got a couple of Christmas cards and that's about it."

"Do you know where the Christmas cards were sent from?" asks Lucy.

"The name Duncan sticks in my mind," says Herman. "It might be something Jacob said one time when we were walking dogs, or over coffee, or something. We saw him and Carlotta quite often—you know, neighbourhood gatherings and such. But they both passed away some time ago."

"Would you have any old photos that I could use if I tried to track Mildred down in BC?" asks Charlotte.

"We can look," says Edith. "We're not great photographers, but there might be something. I don't suppose a school photo would help?"

"You know what?" Herman says. "We had that group photo taken in the park when they were opening the new off-leash area. I think I put it in a drawer somewhere. Mildred was definitely there; she and her dad helped push the off-leash area through Council."

Something goes click in Charlotte's head. "Mildred was a dog person?" she asks.

"Oh absolutely," both Schmidts reply in unison. Edith continues, "She never went anywhere without her dog—or dogs, actually—she was absolutely crazy about them."

Charlotte gives Lucy a glance, which Lucy interprets as an indication that something important has happened. "If you could find that picture, I would love to borrow it and have a copy made," she says to Herman. She doesn't really need the picture now, but it would look strange if they were to leave without accepting the one piece of information that the Schmidts have so kindly offered. Herman goes to look and, after a few minutes in which Edith tries unsuccessfully to persuade the visitors to have tea, comes up with a slightly grubby group photograph. Charlotte recognizes Mildred immediately. She is exactly as she remembers her on her infrequent visits to her home on East 33rd Street—and she's nothing like the woman she is now living with.

In the car, Charlotte lets out an involuntary expletive then explains to Lucy that the puzzle is solved. "Luce, the woman I am living with hates dogs and is allergic to them. Also, she is nothing like the real Mildred we saw in the photo. The woman at home is a fake. What in God's name do I do?"

"Well, what we have seems to be a case of stolen identity, but without more to go on it's hardly a matter for the police."

"But why, and who is she, and where on earth is the real Mildred? I can't simply go home and say to what's-her-name 'who are you, and why are you pretending you're my aunt?'. I'm scared, Luce."

"I think," says Lucy in a down-to-earth voice, "that someone has to find Mildred, or at least find out where she is and why this woman pretends to be her. Meanwhile, you are in no danger staying where you are. And now we should get that photo copied and give the original back to Herman."

They stop in at Lucy's office and scan and print four copies of the photo, and then Charlotte drives Lucy home and returns the original to the Schmidts. Herman says, "Let us know if you find Mildred, and give her our best wishes."

Charlotte thanks them and sets off home, expecting to get there by dinnertime. What she is going to do next she has no idea, but as she makes her way north a comforting thought makes its way into her head: *maybe Leonard can suggest something—after all, he is the one who first thought there was something strange about "Mildred," and he is a lawyer.*

# Chapter 12

THE phone rings at the Stevenson residence as they are finishing breakfast. "It's for you, dear," says Shirley. "Sounds like your girlfriend what's-her-name." Leonard picks up the phone "Morning, how are things? Today? Okay, be there at eleven—see you."

He hangs up. "Charlotte wants to see me about something. Must be the right-of way. We're meeting for coffee at eleven."

"Careful, Len, you may get addicted—and I don't mean to coffee." Shirley is not the suspicious or jealous type, but she is a woman.

Leonard's favourite café is crowded and what Charlotte has to discuss is definitely not for the public ear. She and Leonard take their coffee cups to a bench at Lakeview Park.

"Leonard, remember what we were discussing a while ago—you know, about Mildred and her strange behaviour? Well, I've discovered something rather worrying, and I don't know what to do—she's not my Aunt Mildred at all."

Charlotte describes her suspicions and the reasons for them and then recounts her visit to Hamilton and the astonishing outcome. Leonard listens as patiently as he can, but explodes when she comes to the photograph and the canine finale. "My God, Charlotte, you've got a real mystery here. But it certainly adds up. She obviously doesn't want to attract attention and run the risk of being caught out by someone who knew Mildred. She doesn't want to sign anything more than she has to. She probably has Mildred's birth certificate and SIN card. But, wow, what a mess. Basically, she has stolen Mildred's identity."

Charlotte agrees. "But what do I do? Do I go on living with her and pretending she's my aunt? I don't like the thought of confronting her, and anyway, I have no proof. And what worries me the most is . . . where is Aunt Mildred?"

"I agree—that's the most important thing. And we shouldn't do anything hastily." Leonard has used the word "we" unconsciously, and it is not missed by Charlotte.

The two of them review the facts carefully.

One: "Mildred" must know Mildred well in order to have assumed her identity.

Two: She must have a reason for becoming "Mildred."

Three: She has spent a lot of money on the house and appears anxious to live there. Could it be Mildred's money?

Four: She must have title to the property in order to get a building permit.

Five: Mildred must be unaware of the identity switch or have aided it. Or, a bleak thought—is Mildred still alive?

Leonard undertakes to find the answer to number four. Charlotte agrees to go through "Mildred's" papers, credit cards, driver's licence, etc. when a chance presents itself. But answering the other questions means going to British Columbia.

"Didn't you say Mildred went to BC with her partner?" asks Leonard. "If we could locate him, we might get closer to the truth."

"I'll call Edith Schmidt and see if she has any idea who Mildred was seeing," says Charlotte.

Charlotte feels better having talked to Leonard and decides not to make any abrupt changes in her living arrangements. They agree not to telephone each other more than necessary, and to meet at the park when they have something to discuss.

Leonard is much more concerned than Charlotte appears to be about the potential seriousness of the situation. Theft, whether of identity or property, is a criminal offence and criminals are known to be dangerous when cornered. He has been worried for some time about Charlotte's association with a woman who, to say the least, is unreasonable and stubborn. The only good thing he could say about her was that she was Charlotte's aunt. Now he cannot even say that. But, until they have more to go on, he believes that the best action is to proceed slowly and carefully. He wonders why he is taking such a personal interest in this affair. Is it because of the injustice of building a house across the River Trail? That still rankles. But, no, it all goes back to the face in the window—a lonely, vulnerable face. The owner of that face is in trouble and has asked him to help. All Leonard's gallant instincts are aroused and he is determined to straighten this matter out.

The next day, still full of determination, Leonard sets off for the Town Hall, his destination the Building and Permit Services. As he approaches the office he suddenly asks himself, "What business do I have requesting information about a building permit for someone else's house? They will probably connect my enquiry with my earlier objection concerning the River Trail. And do I really want to raise their interest in building permits at this particular time?" He has a brainwave: *talk to the builder*. Apparently "Mildred" did everything from BC so she must have counted on the builder to look after most of the paperwork.

He returns home and calls his friend Jack Miller, the guy who knows everything. "Jack, help me again, do you remember who built the house on Jacob Way—you know, the one they put across the River Trail?" It takes Jack about three seconds. "Of course, it was Holden Homes, out of Hanover. I remember because I was surprised—Holden usually does developments like golf courses, not custom homes."

Leonard thanks him and looks up Holden Homes in the Owen Sound and Region directory. They have a big ad in the Yellow Pages and the name of the man to contact in Sales. It is not what Leonard expected. If it had been a small, local contractor he might have dealt with him on a confidential basis—such as, "I don't want this to get back to the owner, but I have a client who is concerned whether the owner really has title to the property. Can you help me?" That would not do with Holden Homes. They would get straight on to "Mildred" and all hell would break loose.

He thinks, *why would "Mildred" want to hire a big developer to build one house*? The answer might be that she is really planning to build a lot of houses. That would square with Charlotte's earlier discussion with "Mildred" over real estate agents. No, he would have to use a different approach—a more dangerous one. He dials the Administration number for Holden Homes.

"This is the Building and Permit department in Orchard Bay. We don't seem to have a copy of the deed for the property on Jacob Way. Did the owner file one or did you? We have had no contact with the owner."

"She asked us to file it, and I'm sure we did," Holden replies. "The owner lives in BC. She told us she was planning to develop the whole property."

"The property is registered under Jacob Prosser—all twenty acres. Was title transferred to Mildred Prosser?"

"Wait a moment—yes, we have the transfer, dated 2004. You should have a copy of that too."

"I'll double-check—they must have got in a wrong folder. If I can't find them I'll call you back."

Leonard, with this bit of subterfuge, now knows that "Mildred" is in possession of Mildred's documents and, furthermore, that she has plans to become a developer.

Charlotte, meanwhile, has called Edith Schmidt and finds that Mildred had no serious boyfriends while living on East 33rd Street.

She and Leonard arrange to meet in Lakeview Park the following day.

# Chapter 13

SWANS seldom winter in this part of Lake Huron, but the past winter was a mild one and a pair toughed it out, giving birth to two cygnets, now a few weeks old. While Leonard and Morgan make their way to their meeting with Charlotte, the mother swan and two offspring are moving in their stately way close to the shore. Morgan knows about birds. For example, he has learned to avoid Canada geese, but common seagulls are fair game. He barks and they fly away. Swans are a bit of an enigma. They do not attack, as Canada geese are prone to do—they ignore him, and their aloofness is a bit unnerving. He chooses to stay close to Leonard.

*This is an important meeting,* thinks Leonard. *We have almost incontrovertible evidence that "Mildred" is posing as Mildred and, furthermore, that she is in possession of Mildred's legal documents. Is it time to confront her, or would that put the real Mildred in an awkward, or even dangerous, position?*

He discusses this with Charlotte who agrees that until they locate her aunt they should not rock the boat, but that she should tread carefully with "Mildred" on matters of property and real estate.

As the two sit on the park bench watching the swans proudly, but rapidly, sailing into the distance, Leonard makes up his mind. "I think I should go to BC and look for Mildred," he says. "Shirley and I need a holiday, our daughter Kitty lives in Victoria, and we haven't seen her for ages. I can do some checking around, legitimately, on your behalf. Unless she has died I'm sure I can find her."

"What if she is living under an assumed name?" asks Charlotte.

"Unless she did that as soon as she arrived in BC there still should be some record of her in government files."

Charlotte is astonished that Leonard would consider doing this for an almost-stranger, and says so. She is not an emotional person but her voice is unsteady when she replies, "Len, I can't let you do this."

"Think of it as my job. I've been doing this sort of thing all my life." This is not exactly true, but it makes Charlotte feel better. She thinks of offering to go herself, but there are reasons this is not practical: one, "Mildred" would want to know where she's going and smell a rat; and two, she can't afford it. She thanks Leonard and hugs him briefly.

Leonard brings the subject up as soon as he arrives home. "Shirl, I've been thinking, we need a holiday and I have some business to do in Victoria. Will you come with me? We can stay with Kitty."

Suggestions like this, coming out of the blue, are not uncommon in the Stevenson household. Shirley remembers Leonard giving her four hours to pack a bag for Tel Aviv, where he had decided to interview a possible junior partner. And that was when Shirley had kids to deal with; but she still went. Now she is virtually free of responsibilities, but she is also nearly thirty years older and is a member of a duplicate bridge group that frowns on substitutes. She and Kitty are not close, especially since Kitty took up with a musician with whom she is probably living. She is curious about the "business" that Leonard has in British Columbia. "This is not something to do with that right-of-way thing, is it Len?" she asks.

"Well, kind of," says Leonard.

"And you're not being paid," says Shirley.

"No, I'm doing this because I want to. If I'm successful I may get expenses down the road, but I can't count on it."

This is a familiar story—one that Shirley has learned to accept as part of her life with Leonard, of whom she is very fond. But each time, it tugs a bit at her loyalty and, maybe, their closeness.

"Go by yourself, Len," she says. "I'm busy here. The airfare is a whole bunch. You'll be better off on your own. Just don't dare take that Charlotte girl with you."

# CHAPTER 14

DIRECT flights from Toronto to Victoria are few. Mostly they land in Vancouver and disgorge all but a handful of government employees, tourists, and Islanders. You can tell the latter because they wear things like berets, shawls, and jackets with a million pockets; and show little interest in anyone but themselves. They also carry baskets or leather holdalls instead of suitcases. Leonard is different. You can tell he is none of the above because he wears a sports jacket, a turtleneck shirt and grey flannels, and wheels an ordinary suitcase.

Getting off at Sidney (Victoria does not boast an airport—land is too expensive), he calls his daughter Kitty on his cellphone. "Hi sweetie, your Dad's here at the airport—did you get my email?"

"Actually no, Dad. What brings you to this part of the world?" Kitty answers.

"Long story, Kit, wait till I see you. Can you put me up for a few days?"

"Dad, I am living with Randy, but you're welcome to use my apartment." Leonard notes the "living with Randy", not "living with Randy *now*." There's a bit more permanence, he thinks, in the wording. He's glad Shirley did not come with him. Randy plays in a band called "Never Wed" which seems to Leonard a strange name to call a band—not popular for wedding parties, he thinks. "Ever Wed" might be better, though wives might take that the wrong way.

Kitty's apartment is fairly central and close to where she works: the Royal Victoria Museum on Belleville Street. Randy's place is a rented house on Highway 14, on the road to Sooke, at least an hour's drive to Belleville Street. He shares the house with several other members of the band. Leonard knows Victoria fairly well and Kitty's apartment would be convenient for visiting several of the government offices he thinks might have information he wants.

"If that's okay, Kit, I'll take you up on that. How do I get the key?"

"Dad, I can meet you there. I leave my office in half an hour and it'll take you that long to get down from Sidney."

Leonard takes the airport shuttle, followed by a taxi, and gets to the apartment a few minutes after Kitty. They hug. "Nice to see you, Dad, sorry I wasn't expecting you. I'm bad about emails. Mostly phone or messaging with my friends. Are you staying long?"

Leonard has no idea how long. He might be able to locate Mildred easily, but he is determined to talk to her and get things really sorted out before returning home. He gives Kitty a brief account of the problem, and this both astounds and worries her. "But Dad, you could be getting into something really nasty. If someone has stolen Mildred's identity, it must be for a reason, and I can't think of one that isn't illegal—or even dangerous."

"You're right," answers Leonard, "but I'll be careful, I promise. Now, tell me . . ." Kitty pours Leonard a glass of wine and they chat for a while. Kitty explains that she is really fond of Randy and he's only doing this band thing in between jobs as a mountaineering guide. They are living near Sooke because the band has a contract with a pub there. Leonard can't quite get his head around this, but his policy has always been to let the kids make their own decisions. Kitty's apartment is strewn with her belongings but she makes room for his things; he'll sleep in her room until she moves back in. There's a restaurant a block away and Leonard decides to eat out. Kitty is in a hurry to get back to Randy's place.

Leonard has been doing some serious thinking on his journey out, and has decided that the first approach should be with the Ministry of

Health. Mildred cannot have lived in British Columbia for twenty or so years without a health card. He looks up the address on Blanshard Street, which is not too far to walk. He goes to Enquiries and states his problem to the efficient-looking woman at the desk.

"My name is Leonard Stevenson. I have been engaged by a Charlotte Prosser in Ontario to try and find the whereabouts of her aunt who moved to BC about twenty years ago. She has not heard from her and is worried that she may be sick or even passed away."

The woman is not certain how to handle this. Most enquiries have to do with getting a new card or changing an address.

"I'll check with my manager," she says.

Leonard is ushered into an office and told to wait. A man eventually comes in and introduces himself as being in Public Relations. Leonard explains the story again and produces his card, which shows him to be a Barrister and Solicitor.

"Do you have this Ms. Prosser's written authority to act for her?" the man asks. Leonard has prepared himself for this and produces a letter from Charlotte. "This is not a police case, is it?" asks the official. "Certainly not," replies Leonard, hoping this is the right answer.

The man leaves for a minute or two then returns with a stern-looking woman clutching what looks like an iPad.

"We do have a Mildred Prosser on our enrolment list," she says without introduction. "She drew benefits fairly regularly until about a year and a half ago, then she simply disappeared from our screen. She did not renew her card when it was due—let's see—last February. We have sent reminders to her last address, but they have been returned. On death we are supposed to be informed." She states this last fact with a thrusting out of the jaw; she is clearly aggrieved by the thought that someone should die without informing her.

Leonard says, "I would be very grateful if you would let me have the address on record. I would like to go there and ask around."

"I can do that, but wouldn't it be simpler to go to the Vital Statistics Agency down the hall, and check if she has passed away?" The woman seems to be trying to help, and Leonard agrees to do that but would like to have the address anyway. The address is in Duncan, about sixty kilometres north of Victoria, and the same place that she wrote from to her friend Edith when she first moved to BC.

As Charlotte discovered in Ontario, death certificates are not available without due process, but Leonard is now acting officially and he is able to determine that no one by the name of Mildred Prosser has died in BC in the past twenty years.

"There is nothing for it," he says to himself. "I have to go to Duncan and poke around."

Duncan, a town of only five thousand or so residents, started off as a lumber, fishing, and mining community. It is the unofficial capital of the Cowichan Region, a name derived from the Salish Nation word for "the warm lands." Its warmth, location (close to the Gulf but not besieged by tourists), and proximity to Victoria all help make Duncan a popular retirement destination.

Leonard thinks it time to rent a car. He does not know where his search will take him and, besides, he would like to do some exploring in the famous Cowichan Valley. He picks up a compact Nissan Sentra, calls Kitty and arranges to leave the key with a neighbour, and sets off on the short journey on the Trans-Canada Highway to Duncan. There, he locates the Best Western Cowichan Valley, checks in, and with the help of the front desk, finds his way to the address given to him by the Ministry of Health. Number 3 Clair Street is a small, plain bungalow on the outskirts of town, on a street with only five other houses. Assured by the truth of his story about looking for the aunt of a client, he knocks on the front door. An elderly man answers.

"My name is Leonard Stevenson. I'm trying to locate a Mildred Prosser, who I believe lived here some years ago."

"Sorry, can't help you," says the man. "Just moved here a year ago. Bought the place from a real estate company—I gather it had been on the market for some time." He hesitates. "You might try the Davises next door—they've been here quite a few years, I believe."

Leonard thanks him, walks to Number 5 and rings the doorbell. This time a woman answers. She listens to his story, introduces herself as Carol Davis, and invites him in.

"You better have a seat," she says. "This may take a bit of time." She then launches into a story that at the same time relieves and astonishes Leonard. Apparently two women lived at Number 3: Mildred Prosser and her partner Agnes Willoughby. Both were schoolteachers and taught at Cowichan Christian School only two blocks away. They had lived there before Carol and her husband moved to Duncan fifteen years ago. Mildred, "much the nicer of the two," suffered periodic bouts of depression and quit teaching about four years ago. She spent most of her time indoors and the Davises rarely saw her.

"Agnes was a loud-mouthed woman who did not treat her partner well. We avoided her as best we could. But we were really fond of Mildred. She had a little dog, a Corgi I think, who liked to play with our mutt Rufus. Agnes did not like dogs and it was a sore point between them. During the last year or two Mildred became increasingly withdrawn and forgetful—almost like she had Alzheimer's. Then suddenly she left and we never saw her again. We asked Agnes, who was quite rude, and told us she was ill and was in some home or other. She would not elaborate. We asked around and nobody knew anything more than we did."

The news that Mildred's partner was a woman opens Leonard's eyes to a startling possibility. "Could the fake Aunt Mildred be the partner, and if so, where is Mildred now?"

"What happened to this Agnes woman?" he asks.

"She stayed for several months then moved out and put the house up for sale. Got rid of all the furniture, too. Quite a business that was. Must have quit her job at the school. Can't think why they hired her in the first place. We heard that she had gone east, but no one has seen or heard from her, as far as I know. Good riddance, most of us say."

Leonard takes an envelope out of his pocket and produces the photo of Mildred that Charlotte obtained from the Schmidts in Hamilton.

"Is this a picture of Mildred?" he asks.

"It certainly is," answers Carol, "she was a lot younger then. Different dog, too."

Leonard crosses his fingers and asks, "Do you by any chance have a photo of either of them?"

"May have, somewhere—Mildred for sure. My husband keeps hundreds of photos in his computer. I can ask him when he comes back from work. What do you want to see Agnes for?"

"She must know where Mildred is, and I may be able to apply a little persuasion," says Leonard. "Meanwhile, I'll try at the school. They must have photos of their teachers." He thanks Carol for her help and asks her to call him if she finds a photo or learns anything that might help him in his search.

Cowichan Christian School treats Leonard as a potential benefactor, but loses interest when he explains his mission. Apparently Agnes left without giving notice and without providing a forwarding address. However, they do provide him with a copy of a recent school calendar, which has small, head-and-shoulder portraits of current staff members. This is sufficient to confirm his suspicion that Agnes Willoughby, history and English teacher, junior grades, is indeed the bogus Mildred Prosser.

Leonard returns to his hotel and takes his lunch in the bar. Choosing from a good selection of local ales helps take his mind off the new and troubling turns that his journey is taking him down. Should he immediately phone Charlotte and tell her that "Mildred" is really her aunt's gay partner, and that it seems likely that she has appropriated not only Mildred's identity but also her estate? What possible trouble might this cause? On the other hand, knowing Mildred's whereabouts and state of health could influence the next course of action. He decides to go on with his hunt for another day or two. As it stands now, it looks as if Mildred has some form of dementia and is probably in an institution such as a nursing home, or a retirement home that caters to the milder forms of this affliction. He does a quick search on his laptop and finds that there are ten retirement homes in the Duncan area (not bad, he thinks, for a town of five thousand residents) and that three provide care for cases of mild dementia.

In his career as a lawyer, Leonard has encountered many people whom he would personally regard as having dementia. He would certainly place some of his university science professors in this category. One, he remembers well, would enter the classroom with a kind of sideways step, avoiding eye contact with the students, go straight to the blackboard, and start writing equations. When the blackboard was full he would erase it all and start writing again. It was a challenge to keep up with him. The fact that he gave the whole class a passing mark did nothing to allay Leonard's suspicion that the professor did not have all his faculties in order. Leonard has encountered many such people in his law practice, as well. He had trouble, for instance, stopping one woman from leaving her entire estate to her budgerigar—so he faces the task of confronting a muddled Mildred without trepidation.

# CHAPTER 15

OF the three retirement homes offering Complex Care in the Duncan area, Leonard chooses the one on the road to Cowichan Lake chiefly because it is the closest. He needs not go further than the Reception Desk to learn that Mildred Prosser is a resident and has been a resident for several years. When he asks if she can be visited by someone who is a close friend of Mildred's niece, he is referred to the Resident Care Manager, a friendly and helpful woman about thirty-five years of age. He explains that he is in British Columbia chiefly to locate Mildred for Charlotte Prosser who has lost touch with her aunt and is anxious to renew contact. The woman, who introduces herself simply as Grace, hesitates. "Mildred has a moderate form of dementia, which requires us to monitor her activities and visits. She used to get frequent visits from her friend Agnes Willoughby, but those stopped about a year ago. Do you mind if I ask—do you know Agnes?"

Leonard is unprepared for this question. He should answer "yes," but that might imply a connection with the seemingly unsavoury aspect of Agnes' current relationship with Mildred.

He replies, "I know who she is, but I have not talked to her about this visit."

"Mildred is what we call the passive partner in their relationship, and is very much dominated by Agnes," Grace explains. "When she came to us initially she appeared to be almost frightened of her friend. We gave her counselling, but she remained very nervous, especially when Agnes made one of her visits. Since Agnes stopped coming she has improved considerably. In fact, we think she may even be able to leave supervised care if she wants to. That is the question. She is not used to making decisions for herself."

This is an opening that Leonard welcomes. "Her niece Charlotte is very fond of her aunt and would love to help her if she can. Can I ask you something? Is she okay financially? Does she look after that herself?"

Grace is visibly uncomfortable. "Agnes made all the financial arrangements, and has approved direct withdrawals from a joint bank account in the local Royal Bank. I believe she has Mildred's Power of Attorney for both financial and personal matters. Things are a bit difficult now—we are actually trying to contact Agnes—which is why I asked you if you knew her. We have tried her Duncan address, of course, but it seems she may have moved east."

Leonard feels that progress is definitely being made. "Do you think that Mildred is capable of making her own decisions, given some professional help?"

"We did not think so initially, but now I'm not so sure. Are you a psychologist or anything?"

"No, but I am a lawyer and I have dealt with a lot of cases involving disputes over family issues. Perhaps if I saw her—preferably with yourself—we could decide on a course of action. I could probably get Charlotte out here if necessary. I believe she is the legal next of kin."

Grace seems to be content with this and, after a short exchange with someone on the phone, leads the way to the elevator and the second floor. They make their way down a short corridor to an open door with "Mildred Prosser" printed in neat letters. Mildred is sitting in an armchair near the window, which looks out on a small but well-kept garden. In the distance Leonard can see the outlines of mountains that he assumes are the range flanking Cowichan Lake. "Not a bad home to retire in," he says to himself, "but better if one can get out and about."

Mildred is slight with faded grey hair, and behind her glasses her eyes are a startling blue. She is surprised to see Grace with a male stranger, but does not seem alarmed. Grace says, "Mildred, I've brought someone to see you. This is Mr. Stevenson from Ontario."

Mildred says, "Oh, my room is such a mess—I'll just fix it."

"Don't do that Mildred, it looks just fine. Can we sit down?" answers Leonard.

Mildred gets up, but Grace helps her back to her chair and she and Leonard find places to sit. Leonard continues, "I am a close friend of a niece of yours. Her name is Charlotte. Do you remember Charlotte?"

Mildred looks confused then slowly breaks into a smile, her blue eyes bright with excitement. "Oh yes. She is my brother Jim's little girl. That was a very long time ago." She talks slowly but precisely and there is no doubt that she remembers. "Jim passed away, you know. I never saw Charlotte after we came to BC—at least I don't think so."

"That's what Charlotte told me," Leonard replies. "And she so much wants to say hello to you—she asked me to find you and give you the message. We had some difficulty finding you."

"Is she here, can I see her? Is she a big girl now?" Mildred starts to get up and Grace intervenes.

"No Mildred, she is not here, but Mr. Stevenson will give her a message and maybe she will come and see you soon."

Leonard adds, "She is quite a big girl and very pretty, and you are her only close relative. She would like to see you, I know. I'll tell her how well you look. Please call me Leonard." He takes a cellphone from his pocket and shows her a photo that he took at his last meeting with her at Lakeview Park. Mildred is very excited.

"Oh she has grown—and she looks so like her granny Carlotta—she was called after Carlotta, you know."

They continue chatting, but Grace does not want to get her too wound up, and suggests that Leonard visit her the next day, perhaps for lunch. Leonard agrees. They retire to Grace's office where she discloses that the monthly fee for Mildred's care has not been paid for three months. Apparently, the bank account has been closed and the bank has no knowledge of the whereabouts of the joint account holder, Agnes Willoughby.

Leonard should be surprised by this revelation, but he is not. He has been expecting something like this ever since the fake Mildred's true identity was established. Besides, he is in his own territory now: he has been dealing with matters of false representation, misappropriation, and other fraudulent behaviour all his professional life. It is not true to say he is comfortable with it, but he knows how to deal with it. First, he has to find out the nature of the joint bank account; in some cases there is a limit over which two signatures are required. Closing the account and drawing all the proceeds may be one of these. Next, he should look into the Powers of Attorney. There are definite legal restrictions on the powers appointed to the attorney, one of them being that he/she must act in the best interests of the donor. In addition, in drawing up Powers of Attorney the donor has the option to limit the extent and duration of the Power; and also to agree on how the Power can be terminated. Mildred is unlikely to remember much of this so Leonard will have to try and find the lawyer who drew up the documents. He can see that all of this is going to keep him in Duncan (or at least in BC) for another few days, and he thinks the time has come for him to bring Charlotte up to date.

But, first of all, he thanks Grace for her help and then asks her, "Have you told Mildred the financial situation?"

"No," replies Grace. "The psychologist who has been assessing Mildred has warned us against raising any issues of that sort. She definitely seems to be getting better, but we don't want to set her back. We're actually in a bit of a spot because we can't go on without funds and we have no one to turn to."

Leonard, who normally likes to do the right thing when a damsel is in distress, is cautious. "I may be able to locate Agnes for you. In the meantime could you give me some names and phone numbers? Firstly, the bank manager at the Royal. Secondly, do you happen to know who the lawyer was who drew up the Power of Attorney?"

Grace does not know who the lawyer was but she recollects that the advice of Dr. Ott, the doctor who attends patients at the home, was consulted at some point in the process. This alarms Leonard, because if

Grace has been found mentally incapable, the Power of Attorney may be quite one-sided and possibly irrevocable. He gets contact information for both the bank manager and the doctor and leaves, promising Grace that he will phone her in the next day or two. "And be patient, if you can, I'm sure all this can be fixed up."

# Chapter 16

GRACE has already called Dr. Ott when Leonard phones him. His secretary puts him through quickly and Leonard gives the doctor a short summary of the problem.

"What I would like to know first is did you certify Mildred Prosser as mentally incapable?"

"On whose authority are you asking this?" replies the doctor.

"It seems that the woman who has been managing Mildred's affairs has disappeared, and this has left Mildred and the retirement home in a very awkward situation. I am acting for Mildred's niece, who is also affected."

The doctor seems satisfied. "I met with a lawyer who was concerned in relation to a Power of Attorney he was drawing up. I told him that I had been treating Mildred for some time and that she should be capable of understanding the terms of the agreement. But I warned him that he should explain them to her carefully and make sure that she was aware of all the implications. I have several patients whose conditions have deteriorated since appointing an attorney and are unable legally to revoke."

"Has Mildred's condition deteriorated, do you think?" asks Leonard.

"Quite the reverse. She seems capable now, in my opinion, to look after her own affairs."

"Can you give me the lawyer's name?"

"Yes, it is Grant Sketchly, a partner in Sketchly, Morrison—a local firm," Dr. Ott replies.

Leonard has got what he wants, thanks the doctor, and looks up Sketchly in the phonebook. This next step is going to be more difficult as he is going to be asking for information that is normally confidential between the lawyer and his client—in this case, Mildred. He might have to involve Mildred, which would almost certainly upset her.

He makes an appointment to meet Mr. Sketchly the following day, stating only that it concerns Mildred Prosser.

Sketchly, Morrison occupies the second and third floors over the premises of the Royal Bank. Leonard thinks that what might have happened is that the bank manager referred Mildred to the law firm for advice on the merits of Joint Accounts and Powers of Attorney.

He is ushered into the office of the senior partner. Grant Sketchly is an elderly man with the appearance of someone who has spent a lot of time outdoors. His handshake is firm and he comes quickly to business. As with the doctor, Leonard gives a brief introduction, this time revealing that he himself is a lawyer and that he is acting for Mildred's niece and next of kin.

"What I would like to know," he explains, "is whether the terms of the Power of Attorney allow Mildred to revoke the Power if she believes the attorney she has appointed is not acting in her interests."

"Do you have evidence that this is the case?" asks Sketchly.

"I believe so," replies Leonard, "in fact, I am almost certain that the attorney has appropriated funds for her own purposes. What we need to determine is are her actions within the powers established in the POA, or is she acting illegally?" He uses the "we" in order to assure his colleague that they are on the same side.

"Let me understand this better," replies Sketchly. "Is this simply a dispute over what is best for Mildred, or are we talking about theft?"

"Fraud, I think, would be the correct term. Agnes Willoughby has absconded without notice to Mildred or the retirement home, leaving three months' room and board unpaid, and has closed their joint account at the bank downstairs, withdrawing all remaining funds."

"I did not like that woman from the start," says Sketchly, "which is why I was careful to build in what protection I could, but she had to have access to Mildred's financial assets in order to pay the bills. Mildred certainly can revoke the Power any time she wants, and we can go after any funds that have been appropriated for her own purposes. Do you have any clue as to where the woman might be?"

Leonard thinks it is at last time to come clean. "As a matter of fact, Mr. Sketchly, I believe she has assumed Mildred's identity and is living with Mildred's niece, my client, in Ontario. I have not been able to take any legal action until I determined Mildred's state of health and her financial situation, which is why I came to BC a few days ago. I am still not certain of what legal action we can take."

"Call me Grant, please. What you have just told me is astounding if it is true. How could she impersonate someone who is so unlike her physically?"

"She left Ontario more than twenty years ago and has avoided the places where she might be known. Her niece, Charlotte Prosser, has not seen her since she was about eight years old, but had her suspicions right from the start. Her supposed aunt has been acting very strangely. Now we have proof because I have identified her in a photograph provided me by her employer here in Duncan. Anyway, we know she is not the real Mildred Prosser because Mildred is here and alive, which I did not know until I got here."

Grant Sketchly is shaken by all this and wants time to think. "Would you care to have lunch with me, Leonard, and we can go over everything more slowly?"

They head to Grant's favourite restaurant and order beers before even looking at the menu.

Lunch is a long affair, not because they eat a great deal, but because this is the first time Leonard has had an opportunity to discuss with another lawyer the huge implications of the situation they are in. At the very least, there has been an improper use of funds and an unlawful impersonation for financial gain. More probably, they are dealing with larceny on a large scale and the theft of identity involving personal documents, including title to significant real estate.

The course of action they decide on is first to find out from the Royal Bank (Grant knows the manager) how much of Mildred's financial assets have been liquidated and/or transferred somewhere. Second will be to phone Charlotte and warn her that her fake aunt is really Agnes Willoughby, Mildred's erstwhile partner and probable criminal. She should probably make some excuse and move out of her present home. Thirdly, they should contact both the local police and the Ontario Provincial Police (OPP) and advise them of the fraud and impersonation. Under the circumstances, they are unable to get the Power of Attorney revoked because that would involve informing the attorney, Agnes Willoughby, and they are not ready to do that.

The bank manager is cooperative and they learn very quickly that the financial situation is much worse than they thought. Not only has Agnes been drawing on mutual funds to a far greater degree than necessary for Mildred's support, but virtually all her assets were liquidated three months ago, transferred to the joint account and then withdrawn. The crowning blow is delivered by the manager almost apologetically. "The day before closing the account a very large sum of money was deposited in the account by a firm in Ontario, called Holden Homes, apparently a construction company/developer. That and all the other assets that had been transferred in went when the account was closed. The total was well over two million dollars."

Both lawyers are taken aback. This is fraud on a large scale. "Where is the money coming from?" Then Leonard remembers. The name Holden Homes, the company that built the house for the fake Mildred—they are also developers. She has talked about developing the twenty acres. That's room for at least forty building lots. Lots are selling in that area for a hundred thousand or more. He explains this to the other two men. Grant objects, "But I specifically wrote into the Power of Attorney that real property could not be sold outside the estate." Leonard points out that if Agnes has got hold of the deed of title she could, by posing as Mildred, sell to whomever she wants.

Clearly this is time to pull the plug. But, first, Charlotte has to be contacted. With the two other men attending, Leonard calls Charlotte on her cellphone.

A voice answers, "Hello, is that you, Leonard?"

"Yes, it's me—can you talk?"

"Actually, I'm on a sailboat right now—out in the middle of Georgian Bay—can it wait?"

"It's rather important, I'm afraid." Leonard is anxious that Charlotte knows the full story before the police start asking questions.

"Just a minute—Eric says he can handle the boat. What's up? I haven't heard from you for ages."

"Charlotte, we were right. The woman posing as your aunt is not Mildred. I've talked to her and she's fine, but her partner, Agnes Willoughby—yes, a woman—is the person posing as Mildred, and I'm afraid she's been embezzling Mildred's money. The latest is we think she's sold the twenty acres to a developer and removed a very large sum of money from their joint bank account. I'm here in Duncan, BC, with the lawyer and the bank manager who have been dealing with her, and we agree that the police need to be informed."

Charlotte is too shocked to answer immediately. "But what's going to happen? Will they arrest her?"

"I don't think they will do that right away," answers Leonard. "They'll probably question her and tell her not to leave the area. We think it's best if you move out as soon as you can. You can stay with us—I'll phone Shirley and she'll arrange things."

"Okay, I'll do that as soon as I get home. Won't be for an hour or two. What am I going to tell Mildred—I mean Agnes?"

Leonard thinks quickly. "Tell her you are going to spend a few days with your friend Lucy in Hamilton—there's a concert there or something. It's better if she doesn't know where you are."

"And all my things—what about them?"

"I'll arrange to have them picked up as soon as you're safely out of the way." Leonard signs off and fills in the other two. Grant agrees to call the Duncan detachment of the Royal Canadian Mounted Police

(RCMP) and Leonard will call the OPP in Orchard Bay. He turns to the bank manager. "Is there any way we can find out where the money went after it left your branch?"

"I believe it went into a brokerage account at another bank—TD Canada Trust, I think. She has been transferring money there for some time on the excuse that she wants to manage the funds herself. I'll get the details for you." He leaves the room and the other two get on their respective phones.

Grant arranges a meeting with an officer of the local RCMP in an hour's time. Leonard speaks to the sergeant on duty at the Orchard Bay OPP who tells him that someone will go around to Jacob Way right away, and advises him to stand by for a call from the Anti-Rackets Branch at OPP Headquarters in Toronto. He calls Shirley, who is not pleased at being hostess to Leonard's "little piece of fluff," but who agrees that there is no practical alternative.

The bank manager returns and informs the others that the funds went to a brokerage account in her name at TD Canada Trust, the same account that she has been using for several months.

# CHAPTER 17

THE western part of Georgian Bay, a huge arm of Lake Huron, is not an ideal place for recreational sailing unless you happen to own a cruising boat. Shelter is sparse and harbours are very widely spaced. Eric, a friend of Charlotte's who also works at the library, does not own a cruising sailboat. His rather elderly twenty-four-foot Shark was designed for racing and day cruising in relatively protected waters. However, it can be comfortably handled in light winds by a crew of two, and he and Charlotte are spending a delightful day on the lake doing what sailors do—just sailing around. It is a beautiful day, or it was until Charlotte got the message from Leonard. Since Eric has heard most of the conversation, she has to explain to him that it is urgent that she get her things out of the house. Since the wind is light he puts on the motor and within an hour they are back in the marina.

As Charlotte drives to her lodging on Jacob Way she tries to put together in her head the news Leonard has just sprung on her. She was prepared for some sort of scam, but what she has heard sounds much more like larceny. Arriving at the door she receives her second shock of the day—the house looks like a battlefield: drawers open, stuff lying around, valuables gone from the tables. She runs upstairs. Mildred's—Agnes', rather—bedroom has the same devastation. The second bedroom, which normally is full of boxes and suitcases, is nearly empty. Her first thought is they have been robbed; then she realizes that only Agnes' stuff has been touched. Her bedroom is intact. It hits her—Agnes has flown the coop. She looks around for a note of explanation, or a forwarding address—anything—but there is nothing.

Charlotte phones Leonard and gives him the news. "Leonard, she's gone—taken everything except my stuff—no note. What should I do?"

"I think it's safe for you to stay. She won't come back now. Besides, a police officer is likely on his way over now. Tell him everything you know and give him my phone number if he wants to call me. I'll let Shirley know you won't be over tonight—she'll be sorry."

Charlotte thinks the last statement is unlikely, but the rest makes sense. Leonard tells her they have found the whereabouts of most of the funds and it may be possible to get a court order to freeze the accounts. He tells her he has to make sure Mildred is okay. The bank has offered to loan her the arrears in her rent, but he wants to visit her once more, this time with Grant Sketchly, who has offered to keep an eye on her. "I should be able to catch a flight tomorrow," Leonard says. "Home in the evening, all going well. I'll keep in touch. Good luck, young lady."

Leonard calls Grace and gives her a summary of what they have found out and asks if he can come around and see Mildred once more. "I understand she used to love dogs. Are they allowed in your place? Do you think she is well enough to look after one?"

Grace replies, "You're right, she does love dogs, but the one she had when she entered passed away and we thought she should wait before getting another. It may be time now. I'll have to discuss this with the staff. But of course you can come around—right now, if you like—I'm on duty."

Leonard stops at a florist and buys a vase of early summer poppies, daisies, and marigolds—flowers that he and Shirley grow at home and last well in water. He avoids the popular purple varieties, which he regards as appropriate for the funeral parlour but not the bedroom. He meets Grace who thanks him for his efforts to sort out Mildred's financial problems and goes up with him to Mildred's new room on the third floor. Dr. Ott has authorized the move to unsupervised care. Mildred is happy in her slightly larger premises and delighted with the flowers.

He does not bring up the subject of Agnes, as it is agreed that until they locate her and sort out the finances there would be nothing to gain by reminding her of her friend. Leonard notices a picture of Charlotte as a young girl beside a rather stern man, who may be her father, on the bureau. She must have dug this out of a drawer or suitcase. He is pleased that she brings up the subject of her niece Charlotte without prompting. So many people he knows with dementia have difficulty remembering recent events, and it is only yesterday that she learned of Charlotte's whereabouts. Leonard promises to pass on Mildred's love and best wishes and expresses the hope that Charlotte will be able to visit her soon. He tells her that Grant Sketchly will be here looking after her and that she should not hesitate to call himself if anything worries her.

At the hotel he finds a message to call Grant, who tells him that the Mounties are on the job and are in touch with the OPP. They have told him that they have a number of avenues they can use to locate Agnes: internet banking and cash transactions, brokerage records, credit cards, car, and cellphone. He asks Leonard, "What are you doing tonight? Care to come around for dinner?"

Leonard is tired; it has been a very long and stressful day. He is also expecting a call from the OPP and maybe Charlotte. "Grant, thanks a lot, but I have too much to do, including making flight arrangements for tomorrow."

"That's too bad. I was hoping to get you out on the golf course tomorrow."

"Come and visit us in Ontario and bring your golf clubs," says Leonard. "Meanwhile, let's keep in touch."

The OPP Anti-Rackets Branch calls him and confirms Grant's summary, and that they should be able to locate Agnes shortly. They don't feel they have enough evidence to ask for a court order to freeze Agnes' accounts. Apparently, they have determined that most of her assets are invested in money market and mutual funds, which are much harder to deal with than deposit accounts. Also, it has to be proven that the transactions were not done for Mildred's benefit.

Leonard tells them that he will be back in Ontario tomorrow and available for a meeting at their convenience. They tell him not to bother about stopping in Toronto but to go straight home. They will call him if necessary.

# Chapter 18

THE trip home is uneventful. He is able to turn in his car at the airport in Sidney. He has time to call Kitty and tell her what he has been doing. "Your dad has got himself involved in a rather nasty fraud case—not my usual stuff, but I am quite enjoying it."

"Well, take care," says his daughter. "You are not used to dealing with nasty people."

"Don't worry, baby, you take care of yourself—and I'll try and stay longer next time I'm here."

The flight stops in Vancouver and fills up mainly with people seemingly going on vacation. The business crowd take earlier flights in order to give themselves some time at the office in Toronto. An exception is a large and noisy team of footballers—possibly the BC Lions, though they do not advertise that fact. Leonard hopes they do not have to play the next day.

He arrives home late and finds a note from Shirley: *Playing bridge at Mary's. There's supper in the fridge.* He pours a glass of wine and calls Charlotte, who is shaken but okay.

"The OPP officer came and asked a few questions, then left. I don't think the local branch is too interested. They've turned it over to something called the Anti-Rackets Branch in Toronto. Leonard, who owns this house now? Am I trespassing?"

"No, you are still a guest of Agnes' until uninvited. I don't think that will take long," replies Leonard. "I'll come around tomorrow after you get home from work, if that's okay."

In the morning Leonard gets a call from the OPP. "Mr. Stevenson, we have a dilemma here—do you think Agnes Willoughby will be travelling under her own name or under Mildred Prosser? Her car and all her financial assets seem to be registered under Willoughby. Her bank account, credit cards, and even her house are owned by Mildred Prosser."

"My guess," replies Leonard, "is that she'll shed the Prosser name as soon as she can. You may find that she has a big mortgage on the house and will simply walk away from it. I think she built it simply to create a Mildred Prosser in this neighbourhood. Now she has all the money she needs I think she'll write off what she has left in the bank and start a new account somewhere under Willoughby."

"That's the conclusion we've come to, as well. We'll be talking to the TD Canada Trust branch she deals with in your area. She must be making regular mortgage payments, utilities, etc. We'll see if she is putting money in to keep the payments going and, if so, where it is coming from."

Leonard is not hopeful. "I doubt if that will lead anywhere. I think she is more likely to leave the bank and the mortgage company to fight it out. I'd go after the car if I were you."

# Chapter 19

IN a small town in Upstate New York a woman who calls herself Agnes Willoughby enters the branch offices of the North Country Savings Bank, a branch that serves mainly private customers, including farmers and a good many retirees. She approaches the Enquiries desk and says she would like to open a bank account. "I'm from Canada and am looking for property in this area, with the idea of retiring here." The words "looking for property" seem to raise interest in an otherwise sleepy office, and Agnes is ushered in to see the Branch Manager.

Royce Winters has been manager for as long as most of the staff can remember. He greets Agnes, noting that her handshake is unusually strong, and asks her what she has in mind.

"To begin with, all I need is a chequing account so I can deposit some funds and pay my expenses while I am looking around the neighbourhood. I have friends in the area and may be staying with them for a while. If I find what I want I will need to transfer significant assets to cover the purchase, and maybe open a brokerage account." Agnes knows how to deal with bank managers and she very soon has Mr. Winters eating out of her hand. He assures her that there will be no trouble transferring funds from a Canadian brokerage account to his bank, particularly since a good part of Agnes' assets are in US corporate bonds. She leaves with a debit card allowing her to draw cash from any ATM, and with a solid balance in her chequing account. She gives the address of a nearby motel and promises to keep him posted of any changes of address. He undertakes to look into the transfer of her remaining assets, which she modestly values at about two million dollars US from her TD Canada Trust account.

Agnes is a pragmatist. All her life she has managed to get her way by seizing opportunities as they arose. If you asked her she would deny that she exploits people, but looks out for herself. If someone else suffered as a result she might feel remorse, but certainly not blame. Now, as she leaves the bank, she persuades herself that this is the start of a new chapter in her life. True, she is on the run, but she will make the best of it. On the outskirts of the village she crosses a river, slows the car, and tosses her cellphone into the water. Back into town she buys a new phone and pre-pays it with enough for several months. Then she pays a visit to one of the three real estate firms on the main street and asks them to put together a list of country properties with some acreage, a view, and a new or recently renovated house in the price range of one to two million dollars. She knows that news of this will spread through the village and will add authenticity to her presence and her need for access to funds. She also phones Royce Winters and gives him her new cellphone number.

The village has two respectable motels, several B&Bs, and an old hotel at the crossroads. There are also lodges on the nearby lakes that cater mainly to the high summer crowd. The motel she has chosen is near the centre of town and is frequented by sports fishermen in the spring and summer and hunters in the fall. It is clean but offers few of the amenities Agnes is used to, like an exercise room or a spa. After eating dinner at the small restaurant attached, she decides not to make the same mistake again and makes a mental note to ask Mr. Winters where the best place to eat is.

After a night in a lumpy bed and with a couple in the next unit pretending they are on their honeymoon, Agnes is thinking that this part of her plan is not going to work. Her feeling is reinforced when Winters calls and asks her to drop over.

"Ms. Willoughby, I think you ought to know that the Canadian bank has put some restrictions on the transfer of your funds. There is no problem with the smaller holdings such as your US bond funds, but some of your Canadian mutual funds will have to be liquidated and transferred as cash. The real problem is a large holding of just over a million that you recently acquired. They apparently need to determine the source of this asset. Could be a money-laundering suspicion. We don't have much of that sort of thing here, so I'm at a bit of a loss."

Agnes knows too well the source of the asset. It is the money Holden Homes paid for the twenty-acre property, which was the whole reason for the elaborate impersonation, house construction, and her eventual flight from Ontario. But money laundering? She is shocked. *Who do they think I am?* Thinking quickly, she tries to act unconcerned, but asks if there is a lawyer she could consult if the problem persists. He gives her the name of one in Canton, a neighbouring town, and also refers her to an Italian restaurant in the same town that has a good reputation. Agnes is beginning to think that she made a mistake picking such a small burg to settle in. Canton, a larger university town, might have a bank that is better at dealing with international transfers. At least it would have a large chain inn, with better amenities, good beds, and thicker walls between the rooms. She decides to check out Canton. She can always move there even if she leaves her bank at the smaller place.

The distance to Canton is less than twenty kilometres and the road is fair. Her mind is occupied with the problem over the million-dollar asset. She was careful to invest the money in an internationally traded money market fund that would not yield high interest but should not raise any suspicions from the bankers. The sale of the property itself went very smoothly. When she built the house on Jacob Way she chose a builder who was also a developer so that she would have a connection when she decided to sell the land. Holden Homes was clearly interested in the property, as its location and the fact that it is flanked by a street with all services installed make it a prime piece of real estate. She toyed with the idea of staying and working as a partner to the developer but felt that was too risky. There could be no suspicion about money laundering. It was a clean sale by the titleholder—well, actually, not the titleholder, but the one who was in possession of the deed, and, in any case, has the titleholder's Power of Attorney.

Agnes is so busy working through these thoughts that she fails to notice the car approaching from the rear, carrying the unmistakable signs of a police cruiser. As it nears she can see the lights on the roof flashing and pulls over. A young, sandy-haired policeman approaches her window. "Trooper Brady, ma'am, New York State Police. May I see your driver's licence?"

Agnes takes a thick folder out of her purse and is careful to select her licence and not that of Mildred, which she has been using. The officer examines the licence and asks for the vehicle permit. She pulls that out also. The car is registered in the name of Mildred Prosser. She has forgotten that she did this at the time she switched from BC to Ontario plates.

"Mildred Prosser a friend of yours?" asks the officer.

"Yes, I'm using her car. She is ill. What is the problem, Officer?" replies Agnes.

"Some problem back in Ontario—we have been asked to help them clear up. Will you please follow me to the station?"

# Chapter 20

JUST when Leonard thinks he has done all he can for a while and is happy to have the police take over, he gets a call. "Mr. Stevenson? Detective Solomon, OPP. Is this a convenient time to talk, sir?"

"If it doesn't take too long. I am planning to have a game of golf."

"Actually, I was hoping to persuade you to come to Toronto and help us with this Prosser–Willoughby case. I have been handed the file and it's pretty messy. We have the details of the Power of Attorney, and the Joint Bank Account from the Royal Bank in BC. Also, TD Canada Trust has given us access to the Willoughby brokerage account. But what we seem to lack is motive. You know all the characters, I believe . . ." Detective Solomon sounds as if he could go on for hours, so Leonard interrupts.

"I should have thought that the motive was pretty obvious. Financial gain."

"True, sir," says the detective, "but there are some fuzzy areas. For instance, why the impersonation? She could have persuaded Mildred to sell the land, put the proceeds in the joint account, and then absconded. Why not leave enough in the account to pay Mildred's board for say a year, while she establishes herself somewhere else? Why build a house on the property if she wasn't going to stay and live in it? And why build on the property at all? Why get a niece of Mildred's to come and stay with her—one of the few people that has met Mildred and has an interest in her welfare? What made her abscond in such a hurry?"

Leonard has answers to most of these questions and was hoping the police would get the rest from Agnes. But he is also curious as to why the police are so concerned about the "why" when there is such a clear case of fraud. This becomes clear when Solomon continues.

"There is a feeling here in the Branch," Solomon says, and Leonard assumes he means the Anti-Rackets Branch, "that most of the investments made by Willoughby with Prosser's money could be construed to be for mutual gain. After all, Prosser has given Power of Attorney to Willoughby, so, in theory, Prosser stands to gain if Willoughby does. The police cannot charge a person if no actual harm has been caused."

"What about not paying Prosser's rent at the retirement home?" asks Leonard. He is starting to see a pattern emerging. The police are not going to charge Willoughby if they can get Prosser to file a suit. Then the Crown is saved the time of a prosecutor.

"Failing to pay expenses of a dependant is not an indictable offence any more than is failing to pay alimony," replies Solomon. "We cannot arrest a person for being slow to fulfill her financial obligations."

"Willoughby had no right under the POA to sell the property. That in itself is illegal." Leonard is seeing time slip by and his golf game being threatened.

"We have considered that, and actually Holden Homes is in the wrong as they should have ascertained that they were not dealing with the titleholder," replies the detective. "They could be forced to hand title back to Prosser."

"Do you mean to say that the police are going to take no action in this matter?"

"Far from it. We have determined through the TD Bank that Willoughby is in Upstate New York and is trying to move her assets to a bank there. We have asked the State Police to locate her and bring her in for questioning. We are also taking action to have her trading accounts frozen. We intend to warn her that unless she fulfills her financial obligations, including the return of the proceeds of the sale of the twenty-acre property to Prosser, she is liable for prosecution. We were hoping that you, in your legal capacity, would undertake to help the OPP in those discussions."

Leonard is not expecting this. He thinks quickly. If he undertakes to help the OPP then he automatically disqualifies himself from representing Agnes if she were to be charged for an offence. And he would not want to do that.

He replies, "It seems to me that the problem with all this is that Mildred Prosser, the injured party, has not been consulted; so we have no idea what she is prepared to accept in the way of a settlement. I would be prepared to talk to Willoughby on the condition that I am given the responsibility of returning to BC and determining where Prosser stands. Can you persuade the New York State Police to keep Willoughby in their sights for, say, a week or two on suspicion of fraud? You would also need to get the court to freeze the transfers of assets from the TD Bank for a period of time."

"That is a good suggestion, sir," replies the detective. "Would you be willing to do this for us—on a professional basis, of course? I would have to get it approved by my superiors here, first. Do you think you could persuade Prosser to accept a reasonable settlement without going to court?"

"Yes, although she is mildly afflicted with dementia, so we might be required to involve a doctor in any final agreement." Leonard is relieved that the case is making progress and at the same time excited at the thought of being professionally involved. One thing his rather unusual ethical principles will not let him do is represent Agnes Willoughby, whom he regards as a nasty piece of work. This assignment for the police relieves him of that possibility.

Detective Solomon hangs up and Leonard is still in time for his golf game. The thought of another trip to Vancouver Island is not an unpleasant one. He is going to take his golf clubs this time.

# CHAPTER 21

THE OPP moves quickly and Leonard is requested to visit Toronto and sign a contract appointing him as a consultant. This he does after meeting with Charlotte and getting her approval of the idea of an out-of-court settlement. He has another thought in mind also, and introduces it gently.

"Charlotte, are you happy in this town? Could you be persuaded to stay in this house and live with your real Aunt Mildred? You see, it is her house and the property will revert to her if we are successful. She was born here and has no real ties to BC. I think she is well enough to live at home, but certainly not by herself. You would be taking on a considerable responsibility. But you are her next of kin."

This possibility has not crossed Charlotte's mind. She is happy, and the thought of living with a real family member is comforting. She would not want to make a long-term commitment, but there are some nice retirement homes in the area where Mildred can go when it becomes necessary. "Are you intending to put this as a proposition to Mildred when you go out there?" she asks.

"I would like to," says Leonard. "And you know what this would mean? If the property reverts to Mildred's ownership, she can dictate who crosses it—and we get our River Trail back again!"

Leonard's second trip to British Columbia in a week takes him directly by car from Sidney to Duncan, where he is met by his new friend Grant Sketchly. It is a sunny June day in the most beautiful part of Canada and Leonard's spirits are riding high over this assignment. He has already briefed Grant as to the purpose of his visit and, as Mildred's unofficial watchdog, Grant is happy that things seem to be going her way. He has agreed to go with Leonard to see Mildred the following morning.

"I see you have brought your golf clubs this time," Grant says, smiling. "Are you planning to stay awhile?"

"No," replies Leonard. "Just long enough to beat you. What do you say we work tomorrow and golf the next day?"

Grant agrees to get a tee time but warns Leonard, "You will have to give me at least a stroke a hole on account of our difference in ages."

"We'll discuss that after I see how you play," replies Leonard.

They spend much of the evening over drinks and dinner at Grant's home, discussing the case. Grant's wife Pat is an excellent cook and, like most lawyers' wives, is used to having to listen to business in the evening. Grant agrees that an out-of-court settlement will be best for everyone and is optimistic that Mildred will see it that way. But he is afraid that Mildred will be upset when she learns that her property has been sold. It was left to her by her dad with the request that she take care of it and that it be maintained for public use as long as possible. Leonard's opinion is that there are grounds for having the sale reversed since Agnes did not have the legal right to sell it. Grant himself wrote into the Power of Attorney that real property would be excluded from her Power. An ideal solution for both parties (Mildred and Holden Homes) might be to sever the property into two parts, Holden keeping the north block, closest to the village. That way, Mildred would end up with ten acres and at least five hundred thousand dollars.

Grant is uneasy about the idea of Mildred moving back east and living with Charlotte.

"She is very fragile and sometimes confused. I wonder if she would be up to living in a house with only a niece to look after her," he says. Pat, who has met Mildred, agrees.

Leonard will not give up easily. "I would be only a few blocks away, and she could afford a suite at a retirement home in the area when the time comes."

"But she would not be living in the sunniest place in Canada," replies Pat.

"Well, I'm going to put it to her tomorrow and we'll see what she says."

It is late when Leonard leaves for the Best Western Inn, but he feels that Grant is on his side—at least where the money is concerned.

Grace is not on duty when the two arrive at the retirement home in the morning, and they are met by the General Manager, Susan Edwards, who is more businesslike than Grace. She listens to their story and sniffs. "I certainly hope you can recover some of her money, because the bank isn't going to cough up thirty-five hundred a month forever." She leaves when they get to Mildred's room.

Grant says, "Mildred, you will remember Leonard. He is the man who discovered where you were for your niece Charlotte in Ontario."

Mildred takes a moment, and then says, "Aren't you the man who brought me those nice flowers?"

Leonard concedes that he is indeed that man, and that he has seen Charlotte again and she sends her love. Mildred's eyes cloud over. She is not used to people sending their love.

Now Leonard has the difficult task of explaining to Mildred that her old friend Agnes has been taking her money for a long time and putting it into investments in her own name.

"But is that honest?" asks Mildred.

"Only if the money comes back to you—and I am afraid that has not been Agnes' plan," replies Leonard. "Now she has done two things you will not be very happy about. One: she has sold your twenty-acre property in Ontario—the one your father left to you—and two, she has taken all your financial assets and skipped off to the United States." He puts this very bluntly on purpose, one reason being he wants to see how well Mildred can cope with news of this sort. He is astonished. Instead of looking bewildered or confused, a big smile comes over her face "She is a naughty girl—oh my, my—she was always up to tricks like that. Can we get the money back?"

Here, Grant steps in. "Leonard discovered what she has been doing and informed the police. They have located her in Upstate New York and have frozen most of her financial assets. They are taking a lenient attitude and have suggested that you might consider forgiving her if she gives you the money back, instead of putting her in jail."

Mildred asks, "Is there a lot of money? Maybe I could spare some to help her, if she needs it."

Leonard breaks in. "There is a lot of money, maybe millions, and I don't think she needs a lot of help. The property in Ontario alone raised over a million dollars and she had no right to sell it, because when Grant here drew up your Power of Attorney, he made it clear that she could not sell property. I don't know if you will remember," he adds gently, "but your father was very keen that the land be used for community purposes for as long as possible, which is why he kept it when he sold his farm to Mr. Dean next door."

"I remember Dad saying that he was leaving me a piece of land and that we have a responsibility to the community. He was that sort of person. I told Agnes about it and she was always asking me what I was going to do with it. I was very young when we moved to Hamilton and I can't remember the actual property—is it pretty?"

"Not very," says Leonard, "but it borders a nice forest that has a public trail running through it which comes out on your land. The public has always been allowed to cross your property. I doubt if the developer who bought the land is going to allow that to continue. Grant and I think it will be possible to reverse the sale so the land will go back to you and you can do anything you like with it."

All this is a bit much for Mildred to take in, but she gets the feeling that she is being asked to save the land from development. The broader issue of Agnes' betrayal is of more immediate interest to her. "What should I do?" she asks the two men.

"Firstly," says Grant, "you must revoke the Power of Attorney. That will stop Agnes from taking any more of your money. Don't worry yourself about her welfare—she's made herself very well off. I have a form here that you must sign and have witnessed."

They complete that step, with Leonard and a woman friend of Mildred's acting as witnesses.

"Next," says Grant, "you must open a new bank account so that any assets that are recovered from Agnes' hands can be credited to you. They have given you a line of credit to cover your immediate expenses, which you need to sign. You know the people at the Royal here—would you be happy with that?"

Mildred does as she is asked.

"The next important step," puts in Leonard, "is for you to consider whether you want to take Agnes to court for unlawful appropriation of your funds, or if you are willing to forgive her if she pays it all back to you. We would have to get an auditor to go over all the accounts and come up with a figure for what she owes you. Then we would have to get Agnes to agree that this is in her best interests."

Mildred is full of surprises today. "Of course I will forgive her. It isn't the first time you know—she did this years ago in Hamilton, which is why we went to BC. It was school funds, but they agreed not to punish her if she gave it back. Her family were very upset, but I forgave her."

"Were the police involved?" asks Leonard.

"Oh yes. The school called them right away, and they came to her apartment."

Leonard turns to Grant. "This strengthens our hand a lot—a second offence carries a much larger penalty."

"I hope you're not going to frighten Agnes," says Mildred. "She is a nice person at heart."

Leonard says, "What has to happen is for you to authorize me to speak to her and explain that the funds must be returned, and that you have agreed to drop charges if she does this. I would like to also speak to Holden Homes and get them to return title of the property to you on repayment of the amount they gave Agnes."

"This is very kind of you," says Mildred, "but I can't pay you until I have some money."

"Don't worry," replies Leonard. "I am assisting the Ontario police at the moment, and when that stops I'll be happy to act pro bono—that means without fee—until this whole thing is settled."

Mildred is overcome and close to tears. "I don't know why you are being so kind to me. You don't know me at all."

"I am fond of your niece Charlotte, and she has gotten herself into an awkward situation. Anyway, I am technically retired and I like to keep my hand in. And I like you too, Mildred."

Grant says, "I will draft a letter for Mildred to sign, summing up what we have agreed to today. I think that will strengthen Leonard's hand and avoid any future misunderstandings." He grins at Leonard. "And I'll act pro bono for the time being, also."

Mildred is looking surprisingly chipper after all this discussion. Leonard has a hard time reconciling the confused and depressed woman described by her Duncan neighbours with the Mildred he is dealing with. She does not look seventy-five, which is about what Charlotte estimated—too young, really, to be holed up in an institution. Why the sudden improvement? He chases away the thought that Agnes had anything to do with it. She is clearly a nasty bit of work—but drugs? Mental abuse? He needs to find out more about Agnes' former infractions. Why was she hired by a school in Duncan if she committed a fraud at the one in Hamilton? He remembers that the principal of Cowichan Christian School was a trifle on the defensive when he asked for Agnes' photo.

Still mulling over these questions, Leonard leaves Mildred in Grant's good hands and returns to his hotel to report his progress to the OPP.

"Detective Solomon? Leonard Stevenson here. Well, it seems that we have an agreement from Prosser to waive prosecution if Willoughby returns the misappropriated assets. Conditions are that the exact sum involved be established by an auditor, and that the sale of the twenty-acre property be reversed. Oh! And that Agnes be left with enough money to keep her well."

"Sounds excellent," replies Solomon. "Anything else?"

"Yes—something rather important. Agnes Willoughby has committed at least one previous felony—something to do with misappropriation of funds at a school in Hamilton."

"When?"

"About twenty-five years ago, I would estimate."

"That adds a new dimension," says Solomon. "This might give us grounds for requesting the New York State Police to detain her for further questioning, or even extradition. I'll have to look into the previous case and see where it went. Any idea what school she worked at?"

"No," replies Leonard, "but you might find out from the Schmidts, old neighbours of the Prossers in Hamilton. I don't think they knew Willoughby, but they knew Mildred well and must know where she worked—probably the same school as Willoughby. I can get you their address and phone number."

Leonard is not a habitual liar, but he dearly wants his game of golf with Grant, so he tells Solomon that he has some loose ends to tie up and that he will take a flight to Toronto the day after next. Solomon asks him to drop into Headquarters on Keele Street before heading back home.

# Chapter 22

LEONARD is a golfer whose game, like that of many other players, never actually gets better, no matter how frequently he plays or how many lessons he takes. Some days are good and some are awful, and he has learned to enjoy the good ones and put up with the others. Some of his enjoyment comes from the side bets he makes, such as "a buck says that my next shot will be closer to the pin than yours," or, if he is down, "lowest score on the next hole wins the match." He loves to take chances and will always "go for it" rather than laying up, which does not help his score. Leonard is happy if he gets a few good shots in a round. He enjoys the camaraderie and the bucolic scenery that golf courses almost universally offer.

Today, he is playing with an unknown partner. Grant is probably ten years older than him, but he is on home ground and knows all the hazards as well as the best line to take on every hole. It is clear after two holes that this match is going to be fairly even. The fifth hole has a steep approach to the green so that if your ball falls even a few feet short it can roll back to where it started, or even further downhill. Today, both golfers are struggling to get their balls to stay on the green. Leonard, whose game is suffering, complains. "We have some pretty hilly courses at home, but this is ridiculous!"

Grant carefully places his shot on the back of the green and replies, "Separates the men from the boys."

There is a longish journey in the golf cart from the fifth green to the sixth tee; long enough for Leonard to tell Grant what is on his mind. "Have you thought that Mildred might be in some sort of danger?"

Grant stops the cart abruptly. "What on earth do you mean?"

"I'm puzzled by Mildred's rapid recovery. She was admitted with dementia and she shows practically no sign of it now. She was depressed before admission, and I don't see her as a depressed woman. I'm just wondering if someone was giving her drugs."

"You're insinuating, I gather, that Agnes was doping her so as to get the POA and get her admitted so she could get her hands on the money," replies Grant.

"Something like that—or she could have been in collusion with an associate at the home."

Grant continues to drive the cart. "You bring this up at a funny time—just when I'm winning the game. Is this a ploy of yours, or are you serious? If you are, we probably shouldn't be playing golf but attending to business."

"Let's quit after nine. I'm sorry, Grant. I'm worried and I've lost my concentration."

They complete the nine holes in relative silence, both mulling over the potential outcome if what Leonard suspects is right. Heading for the snack bar, Grant can't help needling Leonard with "This will go down in my records as 'game unfinished because of pain.'"

"If what you think is correct, why would the perpetrator back off at this point in time?" Grant asks.

Leonard has two theories. "If Agnes was acting alone, she would be unable to continue after she left Duncan. Anyway, she has most—if not all—of Mildred's money locked up. Alternatively, if she was working with someone at the home, that person might be alarmed at the attention Mildred is getting from two lawyers."

"If there is a collaborator, the likely one would be Dr. Ott," says Grant. "He is the only one who had access to Mildred before she entered the home. Besides, they would have had to be prescription drugs to have had such severe effects."

"That seems very likely," replies Leonard. "How much do you know about Dr. Ott?"

Grant does not know much about Dr. Ott, except that he has been practicing in Duncan for about six or seven years. Leonard has a smartphone and looks him up on Google. His full name is David Ott and he practiced in London, Ontario, before moving to Duncan. His reviews are satisfactory. He trained in psychiatry before becoming a family doctor.

They agree that the local RCMP should be made aware of their suspicions but, more importantly, the retirement home should obtain outside assistance to review Mildred's medication history. This will be difficult to arrange without Mildred's authority. Possibly, the RCMP will cooperate in getting this done. Grant is sufficiently disturbed by the possibility that all this may have been going on under his watch, so to speak, that he undertakes to start the ball rolling.

*This adds fuel to my suggestion that she move to Ontario where Charlotte and I can keep an eye on her,* Leonard thinks privately. But he knows that he can't confront Mildred with the thought that someone has been poisoning her—at least until the issue is resolved. He will bide his time. He does, however, call Detective Solomon. "Leonard Stevenson here—got an idea that I want to bounce off you before I leave BC." He tells the detective his suspicions and that Grant is contacting local RCMP.

"Serious, but outside my jurisdiction," replies Solomon. "But I have something for you. We have traced the incident you mentioned. It involved a bequest to the private school Willoughby was working at in Hamilton. Somehow, the bequest went missing. Willoughby confessed, but she returned the money and the matter was hushed up. She does not have a police record, but it would affect her sentence if she were to be found guilty of another offence."

"She is not a very successful criminal," replies Leonard, "but I still feel that Mildred is in some danger; particularly if there is an accomplice."

"We can discuss this further when you come in on Thursday. The New York State Police are getting edgy and we need to have a meeting with Willoughby as soon as possible. Oh, and by the way, I have managed to have a temporary injunction placed on the liquidation of assets held by either Willoughby or Prosser. It will not affect cash withdrawals from Prosser's bank account, and we can lift it as soon as the audit is complete and the transfers carried out."

Leonard thanks him and makes a quick visit to Mildred. He tells her that he is heading back to Ontario and that he will be meeting with Agnes in a few days. "I will try and persuade her to cooperate with us and let an auditor go over her accounts. I'll let her know that you are not going to press charges if all the assets are returned. I'll keep Grant Sketchly informed and he will pass on the news to you. Most importantly, don't worry—I'll be firm with Agnes and I'm sure things will sort themselves out." He can't bring himself to leave without adding, "And Mildred, I've been thinking. I wish you would consider leaving Duncan and coming to live with your niece in Ontario. You own a nice house there where I think you would be very happy. Will you promise me that you'll think about it? You're getting so much better, and you don't need the level of care they are giving you here."

Mildred replies that she has also been wondering why she needs to be in a retirement home, but has not considered Ontario. The thought of living with her niece, though, is an attractive one.

Leonard has to add one more thing. "Oh—and you'd be able to have a dog—a big one if you want, or maybe a corgi."

This brings a huge smile to Mildred's face. "Oh, I would love that! I promise I'll think about it. You are such a kind man, Leonard. Can I kiss you?"

# Chapter 23

AGNES follows the police car to an impressive building just outside the town of Canton. Alighting, she is ushered inside and introduced to the Detachment Commander resplendent in what looks like cavalry gear. The magnificence of his attire is enhanced by the fact that he is large and he is black.

"Ma'am, nice to meet you. I'm Captain Lemesurier. What brings you to this part of the world?"

"I've already explained that to your officer—"

The captain interrupts. "Trooper, ma'am—in this part of the world we call them 'Troopers.'"

"Whatever," answers Agnes rudely. "I'm looking to buy some real estate."

"And whose car are you driving? Your vehicle permit says Prosser, but the car is registered under the name Willoughby." The captain continues, "You have entered the country with a false vehicle registration and you are wanted in Ontario for theft of identity for illegal purposes. What do you say to that?"

"I think I should see a lawyer," replies Agnes.

The captain agrees. "I have some names here, but in the meantime we would like you to stay within twenty miles of Canton and report by telephone every twenty-four hours. We will be putting a GPS on your vehicle, so don't try anything."

"How long will this go on?" asks Agnes.

"The Ontario police are sending somebody down and they'll want to meet with you and your lawyer."

Agnes consults the list of lawyers and finds the one recommended by the bank manager. She phones him. "My name is Agnes Willoughby, and I'm just here from Ontario. I'm in a bit of trouble; can I come and see you?"

"What kind of trouble?" asks the lawyer.

"A mix-up over vehicle registration—and a charge of impersonation in Ontario. They're sending down somebody in the next day or two," replies Agnes, more or less honestly.

"Do you have funds? I'm not legal aid."

"I can pay you, if that's what you mean," answers Agnes huffily. She arranges to meet him in his office at nine in the morning tomorrow.

Meanwhile, Leonard has found his way from Pearson Airport to the OPP at Keele and Highway 401 in Toronto. Detective Solomon is a tall, gangly individual—more like a junior professor than a policeman. Leonard could not picture him patrolling the seedier streets of Toronto. But they get on well, and it turns out that Mathew Solomon started in law before joining the police. They discuss what they have found out and where they should go from here. They agree that the desirable next step would be to confront Agnes with an ultimatum. The potential problem with this is: what can they do if Agnes refuses to cooperate? Certainly they can hire an auditor to go over the financial records held by the banks and the brokerage accounts, and they can talk to Holden Homes about reversing the property sale—but should they do these things before talking to Agnes, or after? Leonard is for making a call to Holden Homes. After all, the proceeds of that sale constitute most of Agnes' ill-gotten earnings and the whole reason behind her change of identity. If they can make some progress on that front before facing Agnes, they are playing with a much stronger hand. A report from an auditor will take days or even weeks and will have to be left until later.

They decide that the call to Holden should be made by Leonard, on behalf of Mildred. Leonard has already talked to them, but at that time he was pretending to be a municipal official checking on title and he never gave them his name. "Hello, I'm a lawyer acting for Mildred Prosser, owner of a twenty-acre property you recently bought in Orchard Bay. Can I speak to your manager, please?"

"Hold the line, I'll get someone for you." A minute passes.

"George Reznicki speaking, Manager of Building Development, how can I help you?"

Leonard decides to come right out with it. "My name is Leonard Stevenson, I'm a lawyer acting for Mildred Prosser. You recently purchased a property from her in Orchard Bay. Trouble is, the person who signed the title over to you was not Mildred Prosser, but someone impersonating her."

"Impossible. I was careful to check the title and the identity of the lady who signed."

"Not careful enough, I'm afraid," replies Leonard. "Mildred Prosser is in a retirement home in BC. Her ex-partner, an Agnes Willoughby, has been systematically robbing her for several years using a Power of Attorney, and more recently by assuming her identity. I'm in the office of the Anti-Rackets Squad of the OPP right now, and they have the full details. What we want you to do is to reverse the transaction. Mildred Prosser does not want to sell the property."

"I'd like to speak to an OPP officer, please."

"Detective Solomon, here. What Mr. Stevenson has said is perfectly correct. We are considering charging Willoughby with fraud, but that would delay putting things right. If we can settle out of court, that would be preferable."

"Not for everybody. We have been eyeing that property for years and we have plans to make quite a large subdivision. If this woman has a Power of Attorney, doesn't she have the authority to make the sale?"

"Unfortunately, no. The POA expressly prohibits sale of real property. Besides, she was illegally impersonating Prosser," replies Solomon. "For the sale to be legal you would have to have Mildred Prosser's signature on the title transfer."

"If we reverse the transaction now, we will be out quite a lot of money. We've gone to some expense with architects and planners, not to mention interest on the million bucks we forked out."

"You could argue that Willoughby is responsible for that," says Solomon. "We are in the process of tracing all the financial transactions made by her in Prosser's name. She is going to have to cough up quite a lot of money. In practice, though, the purchaser is normally responsible for checking the legality of the transaction."

Leonard, who has been listening, has a sudden idea. He takes the phone from Solomon. "Mr. Reznicki, would Holden Homes be interested in, say, ten of the twenty acres, at a proportionately reduced price, of course?" He is thinking—Mildred needs cash to live on—she will probably have to make mortgage payments on the house, and she could keep the southern ten acres that adjoin the farmland (and the passage for the River Trail).

Mr. Reznicki takes a deep breath. He has been under fire for committing the company to such a large undertaking. This may be a way out—and a profitable one, too. "I would have to take that to the board. How do I get back to you?"

Leonard gives him his and Solomon's phone and email numbers. "We need your agreement to reverse the sale now, or we will have to proceed with a court injunction. Please understand, Mr. Reznicki, that we are only trying to sort this thing out in the most equitable way."

"I understand, Mr. Stevenson; and I have to tell you that I have been a little worried about this sale. Ms. Prosser—I mean, Willoughby—called a while ago and asked if we would allow a passage across the land for some kind of public path. Of course, I told her that was out of the question."

"Do I take it, then, that Holden is willing to reverse the sale without penalty, or to allow Mildred Prosser to buy back half the property at a price to be negotiated?" asks Leonard.

"Can you give me to tomorrow? I'll have to consult our legal people."

Leonard replies that that would be satisfactory. He and Solomon go over the situation as it stands. The meeting with Agnes should be postponed until Reznicki gets back to them with an answer. Presuming a yes, then Leonard should go to Canton and get Agnes to agree to the audit and to abide by the results. They have no idea how much of Agnes' assets are her own and how much she has stolen from Mildred. This is bound to be muddied by the fact they had a joint account for so long in Duncan. And Leonard does not know how strict Mildred wants to be over the refunding of the assets. Certainly, she is not going to want to leave Agnes penniless.

Leonard's contract with the OPP will be extended to cover a two-day visit to Canton and a day of debriefing on return. After that, Detective Solomon feels that it is up to Mildred to engage Leonard to work out the details. If Agnes simply refuses to play ball, then there are two possibilities: one, if the amount of money (excluding the million dollars for the property) is substantial, then Agnes may have to be charged with fraud; two, if there is only just enough money left to support Agnes, which Leonard thinks is most unlikely, Mildred may decide to drop charges and keep the property proceeds. A million will support her very nicely; even half of that, wisely invested, should be sufficient. Leonard decides to return home and take tomorrow off. Maybe he'll take Morgan and do the River Trail—he could stop in and see Charlotte on the way.

# Chapter 24

CANTON, New York, has two universities and a population of ten thousand. It boasts thirty-five legal firms. It is a historic town, sitting astride the scenic Grasse River, which flows north into the St. Lawrence. Agnes is relieved to find that she is able to choose from a number of good motels, including a Best Western and a Holiday Inn. She selects the Holiday Inn because it is close to the Italian restaurant that her bank manager Royce Winters has recommended.

Her dinner is excellent and her bed, when she finally gets there, is not lumpy. Agnes has the ability, probably through long experience, to put aside troubles and live for the day. Tomorrow she has to confront Dennis Scrivener, the lawyer she has engaged. She does not want to think about this tonight.

Scrivener, Knight and Knight do not occupy rooms overlooking the Grasse River, but are on the second floor of an older building on a corner in the centre of town. She is met by Wilbur Knight whom she takes as being the lesser of the two Knights, and is ushered into a meeting room with, incredibly, a round table. But she is not in the mood for making jokes. Wilbur wants her to lay her cards on the table, which she does—leaving out a few facts like the unpaid rent at the retirement home and the sale of the property. She explains the change of identity as being an attempt to protect Mildred from annoying estate planners, bond salesmen, and investment counsellors. She allows that she has not handled this very skilfully, but maintains that all the asset transfers were done to simplify the estate and to relieve her of the worry that Mildred might make rash decisions with her money.

Wilbur Knight asks a few more questions and makes some notes. "What brings you to New York State?" he asks.

"My attempt to impersonate Mildred was not working. I got word from Duncan, BC, that someone was at the retirement home asking questions. It was probably that nosey Mr. Stevenson who was always hanging around my house."

Knight confesses that he has been in touch with Captain Lemesurier. "You got yourself into a bit of a mess crossing the border with false papers. As far as I can see, that's the problem at the moment. They can't touch you in New York for alleged fraud in Canada."

"Assuming that can be resolved, what can I do about getting my assets transferred here?"

Knight (the lesser) replies that that would be a matter for one of the senior partners. "If you will wait a moment, Ms. Willoughby . . ." He leaves and returns in a few minutes with an older man who Agnes guesses correctly is Dennis Scrivener, as he bears no sort of family resemblance to Wilbur Knight. They shake hands.

Mr. Scrivener is a scrawny man with thick glasses. "Do you intend to stay long in the United States?" he asks.

Agnes replies, "Yes, but I need all of my assets down here if I do, and I understand there may be some problem in that regard."

"Understandably. If there is sufficient evidence of fraud, the authorities in Canada can obtain a court injunction to freeze your bank assets and possibly order your return to Canada to stand trial."

"Everything I took from Mildred's account and put into my name I did because I was afraid she would give it away on some scam or charity. She was always doing that. Also, her dementia was getting worse," explains Agnes. "I have her Power of Attorney, you know."

"How should I know?" replies Scrivener. "But if it is still in effect, it might help in the liquidation of some of the funds. Do you mind if we contact the legal firm that drew this up? We can't help you with assets frozen by a Canadian court, but it will help establish ownership of any other assets you may have."

Agnes gives her consent. After all, Sketchly Morrison has been out of the picture for some time, as far as she knows. Scrivener leaves the room and returns after a few minutes with a somewhat sterner demeanour. "Apparently, you have not told us the whole story, Ms. Willoughby. Mr. Sketchly has a certificate revoking the POA and has evidence that you have defaulted on the payment of Mildred Prosser's bills at the retirement home. Also, you left British Columbia and assumed Mildred Prosser's identity in Ontario in order to obtain title to a deed of land that you could not otherwise sell as that was outside your powers under the POA. Is all of this correct?"

"I am not retaining you to look into all my affairs," retorts Agnes, "only those ones that impact on my freedom to live and move around in the US. Can you help me or not?"

"We will help you with the charge brought by the New York State police that you entered the state driving a vehicle that was registered under a false name. Beyond that, we would prefer to remain uninvolved. I would advise you strongly, on the basis of the evidence we have, to look for an out-of-court settlement, even if it means returning all of the assets you have placed under your name to their rightful owner. This would avoid possible penalties and travel restrictions that would make your life very difficult."

Agnes weighs this advice. She is well aware of the potential problems with the property transaction and the impersonation, and she knows she is on the hook for Mildred's rent, as well as the ongoing mortgage payments on her new house on Jacob Way. She is also, through long experience, aware that she can twist Mildred around her little finger when it comes to sharing expenses. Right now she would like to be able to get in her car and drive somewhere without a GPS telling the world where she is. "Can you get me off this vehicle permit thing with a small fine, or what? I do have a permit in my own name, but is out of date. I have been using Mildred's for some time now."

"Presumably, Mildred's being a forgery?"

"Something like that," she admits.

"It won't be a small fine, but we'll see what we can do," says Scrivener. "Meanwhile, I am prepared to contact the lawyers who are acting for Mildred Prosser and arrange a meeting. Until you have come to some agreement with her, I doubt that the Ontario police will let you out of their sights. If you like, I'll try and arrange this now."

Agnes realizes that she has no choice. Scrivener has already determined from Grant Sketchly in Duncan that the lawyer acting for Mildred is a Leonard Stevenson, and he has Stevenson's cell-phone number. He calls Leonard, who agrees to attend a meeting at Scrivener's office in two days' time.

# Chapter 25

LEONARD arrives home, explains to Shirley that he will be off again the following day, and talks her into dinner at a restaurant only two blocks from their home. It is a small, comfortable place and, as regular guests, they get their favourite table and extra-friendly service. Wine comes very quickly and he brings her up to date on the case he is involved in. "I'm on expenses, so you can order what you want." Leonard requests a small serving of braised ribs and Shirley orders fresh Georgian Bay whitefish.

"Goodness, Len—you acting for the police? I can't believe it."

"Well, you're always telling me that I do too much pro bono work. Can't have it both ways."

"I wish I'd married a man who didn't jump around as much as you do. You're a standing joke with my bridge friends. But I love you anyway. Do you really think you can get this nasty woman Agnes to give all the money back?" she asks.

"Not necessarily all of it, but enough for both parties to live comfortably on and avoid a messy court case. I'm trying to get Mildred to move here from BC. She actually owns the house Charlotte is living in and I think they would get along well together. That would solve the problem of the River Trail right-of-way, too."

"Leonard, you're always trying to arrange people's lives. They don't even know one another."

"True, but I have a hunch. Anyway, Mildred is a nice person. I'm sure you'll like her."

"Len. I hope you're not getting silly about this girl."

"Shirl, I have no designs on Charlotte, if that's what you mean. Anyway, I think she has a boyfriend called Eric—works with her at the library."

After dinner he receives a call from George Reznicki of Holden Homes. "Our board has authorized me to sign a sale-back to Mildred Prosser and to waive claim for damages. I have been instructed to request that the owner consider seriously sale of up to ten acres on the north side of the house at terms to be agreed on."

Leonard is ecstatic. "Excellent, Mr. Reznicki. We couldn't ask for more. Will you draft something for Mildred to sign, or do you want me to do it?"

"Our people are preparing it right now. You'll have it by email, probably tomorrow."

It is still early in British Columbia so Leonard phones Grant Sketchly and gives him the good news. "Mildred can now get her valuable property back, and I'm heading down to Canton, New York, the day after tomorrow to make a deal with Agnes over the remaining funds."

Grant congratulates Leonard and advises him that things have not progressed as well in Duncan. "The police there are unwilling to make a formal investigation of Dr. Ott or the staff at the home without further evidence of complicity. They have reviewed Dr. Ott's available records and there is nothing suspicious."

"All the more reason why Mildred should consider seriously a move to Ontario. Someone in Duncan tipped off Agnes that we were nosing around, but it could have been a neighbour or a friend from the school." Leonard goes on, "I will be talking to Charlotte tomorrow and will see how she feels about sharing the house with her aunt. She can't afford to live there by herself indefinitely."

Early the next day Leonard calls Charlotte and asks if it would be possible for him to drop in later in the morning.

"Morning is difficult, Leonard, but I could take a longish lunch hour if you want to pop in around 12:15."

Leonard and Morgan set off on the River Trail at 10:30 and take their time meandering through the familiar lanes and countryside. They run into a few acquaintances, including a female golden retriever to whom Morgan has developed a particular attachment. Arriving at Charlotte's home on Jacob Way via a newly constructed path skirting the house, they are welcomed warmly and offered a sandwich. Charlotte listens to all that has happened and is completely blown over by the news that the twenty-acre property can now be returned to her real Aunt Mildred. Charlotte tells him that a letter has arrived addressed to Mildred Prosser from a company called Sun Life Financial. Leonard correctly surmises that this is a mortgage bill—probably an overdue one. He pockets it.

Leonard puts off raising the subject of joint occupation until they have finished lunch and are looking at the surrounding land. "What do you think about Mildred selling the ten acres to the north of the house to Holden Homes for development?" he asks. "This would leave her sufficient income and she could keep the south block for public use, or let Marvin Dean go on farming it. The River Trail could easily be routed to the south side of the house or even left where it is."

Charlotte has given a fair amount of thought to her immediate future, but the long-term picture is quite foggy. "I would like to go on living here, Len. I love the village. This is a super location, even if the house is much too large for me. I'm not ready to move in with anyone—though I sort of have a relationship with Eric. Do you think Aunt Mildred would consider letting me stay here and renting out part of the house to pay the mortgage?"

"Yes, I'm certain Mildred would agree to that. But how about her moving in and letting you stay to keep her company? I've mentioned this to her and I think she could be persuaded. After all, you are her niece and next of kin, and she was born and brought up on this land."

"Is she well enough, Len? I don't see myself as a caregiver, although I can certainly help with the meals and housekeeping. As for medication, personal care—I don't know."

"I think Mildred will be able to afford daily help of that sort—even a live-in housekeeper if necessary," answers Leonard. "She is a very kind and gentle woman, and I think you two would get along. She has told me she would want to get a dog."

"Len, could I fly out and see her? This is a big step for both of us and not easy to reverse if it doesn't work out."

Leonard replies that that would be an excellent idea and they should discuss it when he returns from the US in a day or two.

# Chapter 26

The drive from Orchard Bay to Canton, New York, can be done two ways: one (the fast way) is to head straight down the 400 to the 401, then east to Prescott, from there over the St. Lawrence bridge to Ogdensburg, and then to Canton by Highway 68; the other, favoured by romantics and naturalists, takes you southeast, skirting Algonquin Park, then via Highway 7 through the Kawartha Lakes, then to Smiths Falls and south to Gananoque on the Rideau River system, and finally to Prescott and the bridge to Ogdensburg. Leonard, despite the importance and urgency of his mission, is not going to be coerced into going the fast way and missing the glorious scenery of the Shield and Lowlands Ontario.

He arrives in Canton, takes a room at his favourite hotel chain, the Best Western, has a quick snack, and then goes straight to the offices of Scrivener, Knight and Knight. The meeting is set up for 3:00 p.m. and Leonard has been on the road since 8:00 a.m. Agnes is already there and the two concede that they have already met under different circumstances. Also attending the meeting are Wilbur Knight and, to Leonard's surprise, Captain Lemesurier. He explains that he is there to monitor the discussion and to help provide any information they need.

Scrivener leads off by disclaiming any interest with any of the parties—his role is only to help find a reasonable solution to the dispute. He explains that he will advise Agnes in connection with her vehicle registration problem, but will not give opinions relating to charges of illegal appropriations that allegedly took place in Canada. His spectacles are gently slipping down his nose as he explains what he won't do.

Leonard states that he is there representing the OPP, but also at the request of Mildred Prosser who is interested in finding an out-of-court settlement if one is possible. He thanks Mr. Scrivener for his kindness in providing a venue for the discussion and says he looks forward to getting Mr. Scrivener's advice on any aspect of the case that Mr. Scrivener feels it is appropriate to make comment.

Feeling left out, Agnes considers it time for the defendant in the case to make a statement. "I declare," she says, "that I have not knowingly done anything to harm Mildred Prosser who is my friend, and has been my friend for almost forty years."

"That being the case," says Leonard, "you will have no objection to an audit of your finances, aimed at establishing in whose interest the various transfers of assets have been over the past few years. This would include funds withdrawn from your joint account with Mildred Prosser and invested in mutual funds under your own name. It would also include the sale of property under an assumed identity, with the proceeds going to a money market fund in your name."

Agnes has not been following Leonard closely; she seems to be focused on Mr. Scrivener's glasses, which have now reached the very tip of his nose. *If his nose were smaller, they would have slipped right off by now,* she thinks.

"As I said," she repeats, "all transactions have been in Mildred's interest, and you are welcome to have them audited, though what good that will do, is not clear to me."

Leonard continues, "I have in my briefcase an instruction signed by Mildred Prosser revoking the Power of Attorney and asking me to determine by audit what assets have been transferred during the past five years from her accounts to the accounts of Agnes Willoughby, and to take whatever steps are necessary to have such funds returned to her personal ownership."

For the first time at this meeting Agnes is beginning to look worried. "That seems pretty high-handed and, in fact, quite impossible, because for years I have been using her funds to pay her expenses."

"That will all come out in the audit," replies Leonard. "And I should add that Mildred has verbally ordered me to see that you end up with sufficient funds to live comfortably. Considering the steps you seem to have taken to feather your nest, that is a very generous gesture. She will, of course, agree not to press charges for any illegal transactions that may have taken place over the same period."

There is a murmur of assent around the table, and Scrivener, who has removed his glasses, says, "In the circumstances, and without prejudice, I consider Mildred Prosser's offer very reasonable indeed."

Knight follows suit.

Agnes sniffs audibly and says, "Who is this auditor, and how long is this going to take? I'm not anxious to hang around this place forever."

Captain Lemesurier finally enters the discussion. "You'll stay until I say you can go—and that will be when you have paid a five hundred dollar fine for driving a vehicle with an invalid permit." He looks at Scrivener who nods. Obviously the two have discussed the best way of getting rid of her. "And that also assumes that the Canadian authorities are satisfied that this woman does not have to be held in custody. If not we will make arrangements to have her conducted to the nearest detainment centre across the border."

Leonard looks at Agnes. "Ms. Willoughby, It will be in your best interests to sign the instruction that I described to you. If you do, I believe the OPP will waive charges for stolen identity and forged documents. I will see that the audit is conducted properly and that the assets are transferred back to Mildred. You will be wise to keep in touch with me so that you can assure yourself that the final settlement is fair. And we may also need details of some transactions that are not fully documented."

Agnes groans but agrees. "I have no choice—but give me time to read the document carefully."

Leonard hands it to her and says, “I shall phone the OPP now and confirm what I just said about dropping charges. I’ll get them to provide a written undertaking not to press charges if the instruction is followed satisfactorily. And I will confirm for Captain Lemesurier’s benefit that it is okay for the GPS to be removed from your car.”

It was another hour before all the signing and witnessing were done. Knight senior was called on, in addition to another partner whose name had not at this stage found its way to the masthead.

As the meeting breaks up Agnes can be heard to mutter, “I wish to hell I’d stayed in BC.”

Leonard escorts Agnes to her car. He has been thinking, *if this is going to be a working settlement, maybe I should try and establish some sort of communication with this woman, even if she has been pretty awful with Mildred.*

“Where are you staying?” he asks. “Could we meet for a drink and try and forget what went on today? I could give you an update on Mildred and, if you are interested, on Charlotte.”

“I’m not the least interested in Mildred or Charlotte, but I wouldn’t mind a drink,” she replies.

They agree to meet at the Best Western lounge in half an hour.

By the time Leonard gets there, Agnes is at a table by the window, in discussion with a small and rather plump woman who is holding an even smaller fluffy dog and what looks like a martini in the unoccupied arm. “Leonard, this is my friend Myrtle—we met last night—do you want to join us?”

Buying drinks for two apparently thirsty women is not exactly what he had in mind, but he sits down and orders a gin and tonic. The women are discussing the merits of wintering places. Myrtle favours Florida—Pompano Beach is her spot—and Agnes likes warmth and prefers Palm Springs, California. Leonard, who has never been anywhere in the winter except for a week in the Caribbean when the kids were small, feels left out. And clearly this is not the time to bring up financial or legal matters. After a while he excuses himself and retires to his room to do some phoning.

In the morning he calls Agnes' room at the Holiday Inn only to find she has checked out. At his reception desk he finds a message for him. He opens the envelope. It reads:

*Mr. Stevenson,*

*If there is anything more you want me to sign, just mail it to me c/o Myrtle Schwab, 1304 The Grove, Postal Box 1719, Pompano Beach, Florida. Give my best wishes to Charlotte.*

*Agnes.*

Leonard's first reaction is, *this case is moving too rapidly. I hope we have got all we want from Agnes. We haven't even started the audit. What about her GPS*? Over breakfast he works slowly through the steps he will have to take to wind things up, and decides that with the documents they have in hand he and the OPP should be able to proceed without further immediate input from Agnes.

He calls Dennis Scrivener and tells him Agnes has flown away again. "She paid her fine yesterday," replies Scrivener, "and I won't be sending her a bill. We're glad to be rid of her."

"I have an address in Florida I can give you. It seems she has made a new friend. Do you think she should be warned about Agnes?" asks Leonard.

"My feeling is leave her well enough alone. She's on the police radar screen now—maybe she'll behave herself for a while. Incidentally, the manager of the North Country Savings Bank, where she opened an account, phoned me. Apparently, he gave her my name. Some friend! Anyway, he has a bit of her money that was transferred before her Canadian accounts were frozen. I told him the situation. She will probably get in touch with him from wherever she ends up. If you email me her forwarding address I'll keep it just in case."

Leonard says he'll do that. "And Dennis, many thanks for hosting that meeting yesterday. It was kind of you and your partners."

The last thing Leonard has to do is drop by the police station and tell Captain Lemesurier that Agnes has taken off again. "We know that," replies the Captain. "I've put out a call to have her car detained so we can get our GPS back. We know exactly where she is."

There is only one practical way to go from the Prescott–Ogdensburg Bridge to Toronto, and that is straight along Highway 401. Since Leonard has to make a final report to the OPP in Toronto, he grits his teeth and gets set for six hours of utter boredom interspersed with moments of sheer terror. He has never gotten used to the looming presence of huge tractor-trailers travelling at 120 kilometres per hour sitting ten feet behind his bumper. Travelling in the right lane allows him to drive slower, but also raises the spectre of finding himself inadvertently in a right-turn lane and not being able to get out.

Despite these hazards he manages to do some thinking. He reflects that though matters have been fairly well settled, two important tasks remain: he has to find an auditor who will do the messy job of tracing all the Prosser–Willoughby financial transactions back at least five years and decide which were valid expenses incurred on Mildred's behalf. In addition, someone must be appointed trustee to oversee the transfer of any residual funds back to Agnes and to make payment to Holden Homes in return for the title to the twenty-acre property. He wonders if Mildred will want him to do this and rather hopes she won't.

It would be wonderful if Charlotte could be brought in at this stage to handle her aunt's finances. This would entail her going to British Columbia and establishing the necessary relationship with Mildred. His mind jumps ahead. Charlotte is not an experienced traveller. Renting a car in Sidney, finding her way to Duncan, and locating the retirement home will not be easy. But what if someone went with her, who knows the area, and could keep her company? Would it be too much to ask Kitty to do that? On a weekend, maybe? Isn't that what family is for?

In Toronto he fills Detective Solomon in the latest developments. Solomon is adamant that the freeze on Agnes' assets will continue until after the audit. He suggests Pricewaterhouse Coopers as a likely auditor and undertakes to make the contact. He agrees about the trustee but suggests that Leonard should take on this job for the time being. The appointment will be made by the Public Trustee, in conjunction with Mildred.

All of a sudden, Leonard is glad things are winding down. He has been on the go for almost two weeks, including two trips to BC and one to New York State. *Enough for a man his age,* he thinks. Leaving the OPP parking lot on Keele, he turns north and heads back to Orchard Bay via his favourite route—the Gore Road, Orangeville, and Shelburne.

# Chapter 27

WHEN you are twenty-six years old you're used to late nights and hangovers. Kitty, since she started going around with Randy the musician, has become all too familiar with both. She is lying in bed trying to remember what she had been drinking last night and thinking, *I feel like I feel when I don't feel so good,* a phrase that seems to sum it up nicely.

When the phone rings she debates whether to answer it and decides, after the third ring, that it is no good putting it off. "Hello?" she croaks. "Dad? Why are you calling so early in the morning? Yes, I know it's ten o'clock in Ontario, but it's only seven here in BC—no, I am not up and around. Why are you calling?"

Leonard realizes he has jumped the gun a bit. "Sorry, sweetie, do you want me to call back?"

"No, Dad, it's okay. What's on your mind?"

"Well, it's something I wondered if you could do for me," says Leonard.

Kitty's heart sinks. When Dad says this it usually means all plans have to be dropped. "Tell me more," she says.

"It's to do with Mildred Prosser—you know, the case I have been working on. Her partner Agnes went off with all her money, but we have found her and made a deal and it's all going back to Mildred. Her niece Charlotte who lives in Orchard Bay, near us, would like to visit Mildred and see if she might like to leave the retirement home and come and live with her here. I should really be going with her, but I am exhausted. And besides, I thought it would be better if you were to meet her in Sidney and drive her up to Duncan. You are her age and I think you'd get along."

"But Dad, you forget I have a job," replies Kitty.

"How about a weekend?"

"Friday and Saturday nights are peak times for Randy's band, and I like to go with him." Kitty is not going to give up without a fight.

"Just this once, could you miss a Saturday for a good cause and to help your dad out? You could do it two ways: either spend the night at your place and drive up to Duncan and back the next day, or drive straight to Duncan from Sidney, spend the night—I'll pay the hotel—and head back the following afternoon. You don't have to decide the details now. You and Charlotte could discuss it on the way in from Sidney."

Kitty knows she has lost and, besides, she loves her dad and he seems to be really keen that Charlotte should have some help. "How about she flies out next Saturday," she says. "I'll explain to Randy."

"Attagirl, I'll get Charlotte to call you. Thanks Kitty, this means a lot to me."

Leonard phones Charlotte and tells her he has arranged for her to visit her aunt next weekend. "How would that work with you? I think we can cover the flight cost out of Mildred's estate when that's settled."

They discuss some of the fallout from his visit to Canton, and Charlotte is hugely amused by the image of Agnes and her new lady-friend with her small dog making their way to Florida. She is grateful that she will be met in Sidney and will not have to find her way around by car. "I'll call Kitty as soon as I have a plane reservation, and if you give me the phone number of the retirement home I'll call them too and let them know I'll be there Sunday."

"Better wait until I call Mildred and let her know you'll be visiting. She'll be very pleased, I know," replies Leonard.

On Saturday morning, Leonard drives Charlotte to Toronto International Airport and puts her on a direct flight to Victoria. She has a return flight booked for Monday, but will probably be able to extend her stay without difficulty. On the way to the airport they chat about her plans and what she will do if Mildred decides to come east. Will there be enough money in the estate for them to keep the house on Jacob Way? Will they have to resell some of the property? On a more mundane level, what will they do for furniture if Mildred wants to move in? Leonard tells her that the audit has started and they will be able to answer most of this in a week or two—but not to worry, it will be all right.

Charlotte arrives at the airport in Sidney and looks for someone in an orange windbreaker. She is standing near the Avis counter, as arranged. On the way to Victoria in Kitty's old Honda Civic, they discuss Leonard and Mildred but very soon get on to what interests women in their twenties most—their boyfriends and jobs. When Kitty mentions Randy and his group Never Wed, they find a common interest—pop music. She mentions that they are playing that evening at a brewpub on Sooke Road, west of Victoria, and are staying at a rental house on Arbutus Cove nearby. She hints that it would only take them a few minutes to make a side-trip to the pub on their way from Victoria to Duncan, and that, anyway, by the time they get to Duncan, it is going to be too late to accomplish anything that day. Charlotte gets the message and is happy to grab supper and a drink but is anxious to get to Duncan in shape to meet Mildred at 10:00 a.m. at the retirement home the next morning. The idea of drinking until midnight or later, then spending the night at a guesthouse with the band, followed by an early start with a hangover, does not appeal to her. The matter is solved by Kitty offering to drive her straight to the Best Western in Duncan and returning to pick her up on Sunday evening. The condition, they agree, will be that Charlotte spends Sunday night in Sooke before returning home. Kitty insists that Charlotte should meet Randy, and there is an extra bed in the guesthouse.

It is only a short drive to Duncan and Charlotte arrives in time to have a pleasant dinner at the Best Western restaurant. She is welcomed by the assistant manager who, by this time, has gotten to know Leonard well and has had a call from Leonard to look after her and to charge her stay to his Visa.

Charlotte is not expecting guests for breakfast but she has hardly sat down when Kitty appears accompanied by one of the handsomest men she has ever seen: tall, good features, and very blond hair down to his shoulders. So this is Randy! Kitty introduces him. "Charlotte, this is Randy Iversen—Randy, I'd like you to meet Charlotte. Can we join you?" If she had been on a small, shrinking ice floe in the Bering Straits, Charlotte would have agreed.

"This is a surprise," says Charlotte, "I wasn't expecting you till afternoon some time. Of course, sit down." The waitress is hovering around. "Breakfast? Coffee?" They order a full breakfast, which Charlotte tells the waitress to charge to her room.

Kitty explains that Randy wanted to come and bring the van that the band uses when they are on the road. "Mildred might like a drive, and it's so much easier to get in and out of than my Civic," she says.

Charlotte had been planning a somewhat different day, but she thinks this might work. "I have a meeting arranged with Mildred at ten, which I think I should go to by myself—I can ask her what she would like to do then. I know she would like to meet you two—your dad has told her about you. Possibly, we could go for a drive and have lunch at some place in the country or near the ocean."

Randy suggests a drive up the Cowichan Lake road—he knows a restaurant with a lovely view of the lake and the mountains. "It's less than half an hour from here, and the drive is beautiful," he says. "Meanwhile, Kitty and I can easily amuse ourselves while you are with Mildred."

Reuniting after twenty or so years is not easy, and both Mildred and Charlotte are wondering what to expect. When Charlotte arrives and is shown into the ground floor lounge she is ready for a frail, confused, elderly person. Instead, a graceful and lively woman stands up from her chair and says, "Charlotte—I would recognize you anywhere! Thank you for coming, my darling." For her part, Charlotte also recognizes the aunt she knew in Hamilton when she was six or eight years old, and wonders how she could ever have been fooled by Agnes, to whom Mildred bears little, if any, resemblance. She has been under some strain for several solitary months: living under a cloud of doubt, then the shock of finding the truth, followed by not knowing what to do about it. Now, face-to-face, both women know that they are not alone any more. Charlotte takes Mildred in her arms.

At this moment, the Resident Care Manager Grace arrives, anxious to meet Charlotte. She wants to have someone she can discuss Mildred's situation with, and Charlotte is Mildred's closest relative. She waits for the emotion to die down a bit then introduces herself. "After you have had some time to yourselves, would you care to join me for a cup of tea in my office?" she asks.

"That is kind of you," replies Mildred, "but right now I have so much I want to talk to Charlotte about."

Charlotte has noticed some sitting areas in the garden and suggests that they adjourn outside, where they will have more privacy. Mildred agrees and, somewhat to Charlotte's surprise, walks quite briskly to the French doors and leads the way to a gazebo, in the corner of the garden. She wonders: *This is the woman who, only a few weeks ago, was in a room on the dementia floor?* They chat about their lives. Mildred is sympathetic about Charlotte's failed marriage but is pleased that she has found a new home in Orchard Bay, close to Leonard.

Mildred tells Charlotte, "I think Leonard is a darling man. Having him look after me has meant so much to me. I don't know how I could have managed without him." Charlotte is of the same opinion, but is careful about introducing the matter of the false Aunt Mildred and all the work Leonard has done to sort that matter out. She need not be; Mildred is not the least bit sensitive over Agnes' betrayal, which she seems to have already swept under the rug. She asks about the new house that Agnes has built on Jacob Way. "You know, that road was named after my father, Charlotte."

Charlotte replies, "Actually, I think I have a photo of the house on my iPhone." She shows Mildred two views of the house, one showing the woods behind and the other a view of the farmland across the street. Mildred says she recognizes the field, which was part of the farm she grew up on. Charlotte reminds her that the property the house is on was sold by Agnes but that the developer has agreed to return it if Mildred wants it back. She explains that Leonard is having an audit done to find out how much money will remain in Mildred's name after all Agnes' improper transfers are reversed. After that, Mildred can decide whether to buy back all or some of the twenty acres.

"I will have to leave those decisions to you and Leonard," says Mildred. "In principle, I would like to see all of it kept for public use. That was my father's wish."

After a while, they make their way to Grace's office, where a cup of tea is waiting for them. Grace is concerned about the dwindling line of credit at the bank, which is being used to pay Mildred's rent and upkeep. Charlotte explains that the audit is in progress and that within a week or two they expect to have a substantial sum in Mildred's account. Grace says she is very pleased with Mildred's progress and is at a loss to account for the big change in such a short time. She seems a little defensive about this, and Charlotte is careful not to express the fears raised by Leonard as to the possible cause of the initial depression and memory loss.

Charlotte feels it is about time to come to grips with Mildred's long-term outlook. "Don't you think," she says to both of them, "that a retirement home is a little too much care under the present circumstances? Wouldn't Mildred be better off living in a house with a companion and maybe a dog? I have thought a lot about this, and I would be happy to undertake the job—as the companion, that is."

Mildred addresses Grace: "You have all been very kind to me here, and I am grateful. But it has not really been a happy place for me, especially recently. I know that is not your fault, and I should have known that Agnes was not fond of me." Here she breaks down and covers her face. Charlotte goes to her and puts her arm around her shoulders.

"That's over, Aunt Mildred. She won't bother you again; Leonard and I'll see to it."

Charlotte tells Mildred that Leonard's daughter Kitty and her boyfriend are here from Victoria and would like to say hello. "Also, they have a nice van and would like to take us for a drive—if you feel like it. We could go somewhere and maybe have lunch. I think you will like Kitty—in a way, she is a bit like Leonard." This is reaching a bit far, but Kitty does have the same interest in the environment as Leonard. Mildred cheers up quickly and looks at Grace to see how she is reacting to this.

"I think that would be okay," Grace says. "And as for leaving the home, we are always happy when our residents are well enough to manage on their own. But I'm not sure if Mildred is ready for that—she will need a companion or full-time housekeeper. Are you certain you're up to that, Charlotte?"

"I've done a lot of thinking, and that's one reason I came out here. I'm sure now. Anyway, we can't do any moving until the funds are transferred and, besides, there really isn't much furniture. Agnes only camped there, and anything moveable she took with her. There's a bed and a dresser—that's about it."

Mildred says, "That's quite enough to start with. You and I can have fun buying things together. Now, I would really like to go for that drive."

As if on cue, a tall, blond person comes in the door. All but Charlotte assume it to be Leonard's niece Kitty. "I'm Randy," says the person. "Kitty's outside in the van." The discussion ends and Charlotte and Mildred follow Randy to the car. Grace looks wistful, possibly at the prospect of losing Mildred—but more likely because she wouldn't mind going in the van with this gorgeous man.

They elect to do the drive to Cowichan Lake, a trip of about thirty kilometres through some of the most spectacular scenery on Vancouver Island. Mildred says she has been there before on a bus trip, but was not feeling well at the time. She sits with Randy in the front, and he charms her with stories of the history of the area. Lunch is on the deck of a restaurant just outside the town of Cowichan Lake, and the conversation is an opportunity for Kitty to appreciate what her father sees in Mildred. "Nice of you young people to spend your day dragging an old lady around," she says. "Of course, Kitty, you must have learned generosity from your father."

"I am here on his orders," replies Kitty, "but, to tell you the truth, I wouldn't have missed this for anything."

After lunch they go for a walk on a footpath near the lake. Mildred remarks that she has never seen snow on mountaintops in the middle of summer. "It looks as if angels have come down and touched them with silver," she says. The high grasslands and snowy peaks remind Charlotte of *The Sound of Music,* which she starts to hum. Instantly, Randy breaks into song: "I go to the hills . . ." and Kitty joins, with Mildred soon after. The melody seems to float over the blue-green lake and disappear into the surrounding forests—an idyllic moment for all of them.

Kitty says, "Now you all know why I live in BC."

On the way back to the car the two girls go ahead. Charlotte is curious as to why Kitty's dad has taken such an interest in Mildred's case. "Is he always like this?" she asks. "Does he look for people who are in trouble and help sort them out?"

Kitty says this is sort of normal for him. "He doesn't exactly look for them but he loves to take on challenges when the issues are important to him. Drives Mum crazy, but I think we all understand—that's Dad."

Charlotte is also interested in Kitty's work with the BC government. "What exactly do you do at the Royal Victoria Museum?" she asks.

"Well, I'm really on loan to the museum from the Wildlife Branch of the Ministry of the Environment in Nanaimo. I'll probably go back there after the exhibit is set up—in about six or so months." She sounds a bit wistful and Charlotte senses that Randy may be the cause of this. Kitty continues, "Before moving to Victoria, I had a job monitoring fish populations in some of the rivers flowing into the Gulf. I really enjoy that sort of work—lots of outdoors and travel. Randy likes the outdoors, too. He was a kayak instructor before starting the band—and before that he was into mountaineering. I'm trying to persuade him to start a business in Nanaimo, doing the same sort of thing."

While the girls are talking, Randy takes Mildred by the arm and guides her along the path, pointing to the different plants and trees along the way. "For a musician, you seem to know a lot about wildlife," remarks Mildred.

"Well, I mean, I studied biology in Oslo before coming to Canada, and then I had a whole lot of jobs doing hiking tours and mountain climbing in BC before getting into music," he replies. Mildred asks why he left Norway and whether Randy is really a Norwegian name. "My name is really Erland—it is a common name in Norway—I left because the winters there are cold and dark and too long, and I am a person who likes light and warmth and laughter. Norwegians are too serious. And you, Mildred, you are too young to be in a home with old people. You and Charlotte should take a vacation and go to Paris and Rome—see the world."

"Don't be silly," she replies.

Charlotte has been wondering about tonight. She did promise Kitty and Randy that she would spend the evening with them in Sooke, but can she leave Mildred now? And if so, should she come back on Monday and talk more to Mildred about her plans? Mildred solves the dilemma by saying quietly to Charlotte, "My dear, I think you and your friends should go off and leave me to collect myself. I have a lot to think about and, like you say, we can't do anything until the money is sorted out."

They drive back to Duncan and Charlotte escorts Mildred to her room. They hug and cry a little and promise to keep in touch. Then Charlotte and her new friends head back to Sooke and to the pub where the band has been playing.

There are six breweries in the Victoria area, as well as five brewpubs, and the Arbutus Pub is one of these. That is not to say that the ten other local brands are not served; or, in fact, the twenty-odd brands that are brewed and favoured in Vancouver. Sightseeing in Duncan is thirsty work and tonight there is an emotional factor too, which makes the first few swigs all the more satisfying. Kitty's and Randy's friends are a welcoming bunch and, although the band is not on duty, they are persuaded to play a few of their favourites. Charlotte, though not exactly a party girl, has always enjoyed an evening out and has missed this in the rather staid confines of Orchard Bay.

Overnight in the guesthouse is another thing altogether, and Charlotte is glad it is a one-night event.

Kitty drives her into Victoria in the morning on her way to work and puts her on the shuttle to the airport. Charlotte makes a goodbye phone call to Mildred, who is anxious to hear how she made out with the gang in Sooke. "Well, thanks Mildred," Charlotte says (she has stopped calling her Aunt), "but one night is enough."

Mildred answers, "Say hello to Leonard and thank him for sending you to cheer me up. I really enjoyed yesterday, and I hope we will be seeing more of each other soon."

On the crowded, single-aisle plane she sits next to a couple of elderly women who order water in paper cups when the drink trolley comes around. As soon as the flight attendant has left they discretely remove miniatures of gin from their purses and pour themselves a good drink. They offer some to Charlotte, but she has finished her Coke and, tired from last night, decides to sleep.

The Simcoe County Airport Bus takes her to Collingwood and Leonard is there to pick her up. On the way home she gives Leonard an account of her visit—leaving out the night in Sooke. He is glad to hear that Mildred is favourably inclined to coming to Ontario, and he tells Charlotte that Pricewaterhouse Coopers is already well into the audit and are predicting a completion within a week.

# CHAPTER 28

ON one of the higher floors of the PricewaterhouseCoopers (PwC) Tower in downtown Toronto two students are sorting through a pile of bank statements, dividend slips, tax returns, and other financial documents in an effort to trace the rather convoluted path taken by Agnes Willoughby in her five-or-so-year effort to separate Mildred Prosser from her money. From time to time they stop to look at each other and remark on the ingenuity required to take a registered asset from its owner and register it in another name. The trick, in most cases, has been to use the Power of Attorney to sell the asset and put the proceeds into the Royal Bank joint chequing account. From there it would, after a decent period of time, get invested in another asset under the two names. Dividends and periodic withdrawals from that asset would go directly to Agnes' personal account at TD Canada Trust. By this and similar means, Agnes became richer while Mildred became poorer. The two students improved their knowledge of finance at no cost to PwC.

Today, the audit (it will not really be called that until a Partner has approved the report) has reached the point where the trail is complete, but there are still questions as to the legitimacy of a few of the transactions, as well as what constitutes a fair division of the spoils given Mildred's insistence on Agnes being "looked after." To do this, the court-approved trustee, Leonard Stevenson, needs to be consulted. The Partner assigned to the audit, Roger Downey, calls Leonard and sets up a meeting. The two students will be required to attend and provide explanations where necessary.

Leonard congratulates Mr. Downey on the speed with which the work has been completed. Mr. Downey assures Leonard that the two students deserve most of the credit and that PricewaterhouseCoopers always tries to provide satisfaction. Then they get down to business. It is clear that Mildred was left a considerable amount of money by her father, Jacob Prosser—presumably from the sale of the farm in Orchard Bay. And on the whole, Agnes has been lucky in her choice of investments. The aggregate of Mildred's assets has grown by more than 30 percent in the past five years, despite withdrawals for Mildred's upkeep and periodic supplements towards Agnes' surprisingly modest lifestyle. It is these supplements that Leonard is required to pass judgement on. He chooses to decide in favour of Agnes in most of these, influenced partly by the surprising discovery that Agnes has named Mildred as the sole beneficiary of her estate in a will drawn up less than six months ago.

Another asset that catches Leonard's attention is a condominium in Pompano Beach, Florida. Unlike all of the other recent investments, this one is registered in the names of Agnes Willoughby and Mildred Prosser. Leonard decides that he will recommend to the Provincial Trustee that a fair settlement would be to forget any past personal expenses but to transfer all assets purchased with Mildred's money, including Agnes' half of the condominium, to Mildred. He will have to get Mildred's agreement to this before making a formal report. Behind this decision is the image he cannot get out of his mind of Agnes and the fat lady with her furry dog in a condo in Pompano Beach—a condo purchased with Mildred's money.

Leonard emails Grant Sketchly the summary prepared by the auditors and describes the settlement he is proposing. He follows this with a phone call. "Do you think you can discuss this with Mildred, or should I make another trip out west?" he asks.

"Let me have a go," replies Grant. "Personally, I think Mildred will balk at leaving Agnes without any assets except what she had when they became partners, particularly since she has named Mildred as sole beneficiary in her will."

"I think you have to discount that," says Leonard. "Agnes can change her will any time she likes, and may have already."

Grant's meeting with Mildred has the outcome he expected. Mildred is shocked by the size of her investment portfolio and suggests that, since Agnes has managed it so well, she should receive the condo in Florida as a bonus. Grant explains that if she were to do that and buy back the twenty-acre property in Orchard Bay and pay off the mortgage on the house, she would not have enough left to live comfortably, particularly if she wants to leave something in her estate for Charlotte. He recommends that she think it over and possibly discuss it with Leonard and Charlotte.

A matter that is foremost in Mildred's head at the moment concerns the retirement home. It has been in turmoil for several weeks, with RCMP officials there nearly every day, poring over books and records and asking questions and culminating in the abrupt departure of the nurse who administers the medications. Grace, who is visibly upset, is filling in at the moment, on top of her other jobs. Rumour has it that the General Manager is about to leave. A number of the residents are talking about moving to another home. Mildred asks Grant if he has heard anything about the situation.

"I have been talking to the RCMP," he says. "Leonard and I were worried that there might have been some tampering with your medication when you were admitted to the home—you told us how Agnes had behaved so strangely for a long time—and your recovery has been so fast lately. The RCMP were concerned that there might be other cases of the same thing happening here. I believe that the matter is being turned over to the BC Ministry of Health to do a full investigation. It will probably get solved soon."

Mildred is distressed by this story, although Leonard has told her about his suspicions. "If Agnes was responsible in my case," she says, "why is it still going on when she's in Florida or someplace?"

"I don't know the details, Mildred," he answers. "It could have been a mistake, or it might be that the nurse that was let go had a mental problem."

"I don't feel comfortable now. There may be others in the same situation as me," she says. "I think I've decided to move, and Charlotte's invitation to move in with her in my house in Ontario looks very attractive. I'm going to give her a call and see if she still wants me. Also, I'll ask her what she thinks about the settlement with Agnes. I really think Agnes should get the condo even if it means I can only keep half the land in Orchard Bay."

Grant tells her she should do what she wants—about the move, and about the settlement—and that he will be happy to help, if he can, with either.

# Chapter 29

CHARLOTTE is on her way to Duncan for the second time. This time she has rented a car in Sidney and is trying to figure out the GPS system. Initially, it took her over to the Saanich Inlet side of the peninsula and she nearly ended up at The Butchart Gardens, which would have been fun to see but is not on her current agenda. She is on her way to Duncan to help pack up Mildred's belongings and take them and Mildred back east to Orchard Bay. She figures out that she has taken Highway 17A instead of Highway 17, but never mind, the scenery is delightful and the two roads join very soon and then she will be on the magnificent Malahat Highway leading north all the way to Duncan.

Telephone discussions over a day or two between Mildred, Leonard, and Grant have culminated in the decision to move. But first, agreement had to be reached over the disposition of the funds and property appropriated by Agnes. In this, Mildred got her way: the condo in Florida will stay jointly registered, but in Agnes' possession; Mildred will regain the twenty acres at Orchard Bay and title to the house, and Agnes will not be required to compensate Mildred for the funds used for personal expenses over the past five years.

PricewaterhouseCoopers has put into motion the necessary bank and investment fund transfers, and Leonard has opened a bank account for her at the TD Canada Trust in Orchard Bay. Legal papers required to be signed by Agnes are on their way to the forwarding address in Pompano Beach.

As she approaches Duncan, Charlotte wonders how all this has happened in such a short time. Events have tumbled upon one another without really being planned. She realizes that Leonard has been the catalyst for most of this, starting with the discovery of the house blocking his beloved River Trail. She wonders what would have happened if she had found herself living with a strange and clearly dishonest lady without Leonard's guiding hand to put the chain of events in effect. All the same, she has a warm feeling about the decision she has taken. She is really fond of her aunt and is confident they will get along together. She is financially secure for the first time (it seems) in ages.

She is also looking forward to having Mildred as company in the big and rather lonely house. One of the first things they are going to do is buy a dog. They will probably start with the Humane Society pound in Collingwood, where she knows Mildred will fall in love with at least one of the four-legged residents. Then they will start looking for furniture, as all Mildred is bringing with her are personal effects—mostly clothes. They will have fun doing this as there are dozens (maybe hundreds) of neat places in the area that sell pine furniture and "antique" stuff of all sorts.

One of the concerns that Charlotte has is: how will Eric fit in? Over the past few weeks they have been seeing quite a lot of each other, and not just during the day. His "home" is a room in his parents' house, a farm a few kilometres south of Orchard Bay. Her house is only a few blocks from the library. Good enough reason to go there, they both think. This will probably have to stop for the time being. Mildred is not a worldly person, but Charlotte thinks she will come around to accept Eric as an occasional houseguest. The house is certainly big enough for the three of them.

The goodbyes at the retirement home are relatively short. Mildred has prepared for her departure and only Grace turns up to hug her as she gets into Charlotte's rented SUV to take them to Sidney. They stop by Grant Sketchly's office to thank him for his help, and Grant tells Charlotte to remind Leonard that their game of golf was not completed and that he will be giving Leonard a call on his next visit to Toronto.

There is quite a lot of luggage to check in at the airport and the excess baggage cost is astronomical by Charlotte's standards. She offers to take some to the freight terminal, but Mildred is happy to pay the premium to keep things simple. They are lucky to be travelling on a direct flight to Toronto and Mildred has insisted on Executive Class. She has not been on an airplane for over twenty years and is enjoying the experience. In fact, Charlotte has never seen her aunt as happy as she looks through the lunch menu and picks beef tenderloin as her main course. She manages to dissuade her from a third gin and tonic despite Mildred's admonition "But, my darling, they're free!"

Leonard has agreed to meet them in Toronto and has borrowed his friend Jack Miller's new Ford Expedition in order to accommodate Mildred's belongings. This it does comfortably and the drive to Orchard Bay is pleasant, especially for Mildred, who is surprised to see the changed face of Southern Ontario. She is even more surprised at the size of her new house and can see that she will have her hands full creating a garden—landscapers are so expensive, but now she won't have to worry about that. Leonard shows her his beloved River Trail and how they have diverted it to pass to the north of the house. *Maybe, if the land to the north is sold, we can move it to the south, where Mildred will own ten acres. There are many possibilities,* he thinks.

Shirley Stevenson has put some food in the fridge and, since it is now late by local time, Mildred and Charlotte have a light snack and go to bed without unpacking.

A day or two later, Leonard and Morgan are enjoying their favourite walk on the River Trail. The swans are still plying the waters off Lakeview Park, the parents looking like cruise ships while the cygnets scurry along behind like pilot boats hurrying to catch up. Leonard is not normally one to reconsider decisions, but watching the swans makes him reflect that events have moved abnormally fast these past few weeks. He wonders: *Am I like the father swan and have I been dragging Mildred and Charlotte behind me all these weeks? I hope it will all work out.*

As he approaches the edge of the woods adjoining Mildred's property, Morgan hears barking and runs ahead to investigate. Leonard takes the trail around the house and looks up to find where the sound is coming from. In the window where only a month or so ago he caught a glimpse of a face which withdrew quickly but will now never leave his memory, he sees three faces: Charlotte's, Mildred's, and the grey, hairy face of a barking dog.

About a month later, Leonard is enjoying his second cup of coffee and sorting through *The Globe and Mail,* trying to find some news amidst the full-page ads and special features when a headline catches his eye: "Canadian woman implicated in Florida brawl." The article (short by the *Globe*'s standards) describes how police were called to a Pompano Beach apartment when neighbours reported screams and loud banging in the building. An elderly woman, who was taken to the hospital with severe injuries, claimed that she caught her partner putting poison in her pet's dog food and when she tried to interfere was beaten badly with a cane. Her partner, who suffered minor injuries, has been taken into custody pending further investigation. The case is complicated by the fact that the partner is a Canadian woman who is under observation by the police for alleged fraud and stolen identity.

Over the course of his career, Leonard has learned to detach himself from issues once his role has been completed. This news, however, disturbs him. Has he been focusing too narrowly on the financial side of the case and overlooked that Agnes is a potential poisoner? He is troubled by the thought that Agnes, who quit the stage bloodied and disgraced, is still causing pain to others—including the four-legged variety. He phones his friend Grant Sketchly.

"Grant, Leonard here. Did you notice the article in the *Globe* about the Canadian woman in Florida poisoning her friend's dog and then beating her up? Must be Agnes."

"No," replies Grant. "What brings you to that conclusion?"

"Pompano Beach, and the fact that the police noted that she was under suspicion for fraud and stolen identity. Grant, I'm worried that we didn't take the drug part of the case seriously enough. What has happened at the retirement home about that issue?"

"You can rest there, Leonard old man. The Ministry of Health did a great job of investigation and concluded that there was indeed an ongoing conspiracy to over-medicate residents in order to charge higher fees for dementia care. Several charges have been laid, and it looks as if one or two staff will serve jail time. I think the home will be closing down."

Leonard is not entirely satisfied. "But why would Mildred have shown the symptoms before entering the home? And why did they stop as soon as Agnes left for Ontario?"

"I have not told you the whole story," replies Grant. "The ministry and the police have also uncovered several cases where staff were bribed by family and guardians to administer drugs in order to render residents unable to realize that they were being robbed. I suspect Agnes started on her own and then bribed the home to keep on dispensing. I know the police have Agnes on their list, and I am told—please keep this under your hat—that steps are being taken to have her extradited to Canada to stand trial. I needn't remind you that bribery to cause harm is a serious criminal offence. She won't get off this one easily."

There follows further discussion of the case and Leonard is happy to learn that efforts are being made to keep the whole matter away from the media, at least for the present. Hopefully Mildred won't be called as a witness, since the staff have made full confessions.

Leonard thanks Grant for the information and asks how his golf game is coming along. Grant promises to keep Leonard informed and asks him to pass his best wishes on to Charlotte and Mildred. He also suggests that Leonard keep quiet about the scandal and Agnes' involvement.

For his part, Leonard is only too pleased to bury the matter. Now that Agnes is safely in the hands of the courts, she will find it hard to continue on her destructive course. In any case, it is no longer his affair. He is content that the journey—which started with his outrage over the blocked River Trail and has taken him along some crooked paths, facing him with several unexpected obstacles and nasty people—has come to a satisfactory end. He also has a welcome feeling that he has met some really nice people and has been able to help them.

On second thoughts, maybe he will tell Charlotte about Agnes.

# Acknowledgements

I WOULD like to acknowledge the help I received in writing this book, beginning with the encouragement of two friends, Don Ross and Dorris Heffron, both experienced writers and (in the case of Dorris) author of five published novels. They convinced me that to start a book at my age was not a dream but a practical, albeit challenging, idea. I think what kept me going during the first few weeks was the interest shown by my wife Sally who would ask me at Happy Hour what Leonard had been up to that day. I am grateful to my sons John, Michael and Norman and daughter Catherine, as well as Dorris Heffron, for their favourable comments on the first draft, and for their very useful and often necessary suggestions. Catherine and her husband Peter also helped me in the composition of the cover picture. I want to acknowledge the outstanding professionalism and courtesy of FriesenPress throughout the publication process, as well as the timely help of my niece Susan Paterson with the final editing and proofreading.

Printed in Canada